FOR WHOM THE BELL TOLLS

Laura Shenton

FOR WHOM THE BELL TOLLS

Laura Shenton

Iridescent Toad Publishing

Iridescent Toad Publishing.

First edition. ISBN 978-1-913779-15-3

Chapter One

The bitter winter wind howled through the narrow, twisting streets of Ryehaven, carrying with it not just the biting cold but the faint, unmistakable tang of decay that had become all too familiar in recent months. Delicate snowflakes drifted lazily down from the leaden sky, gradually blanketing the crooked, weathered rooftops and transforming the worn cobblestones into treacherous paths that forced people to pick their steps with careful precision.

Beneath the skeletal outline of winter-stripped trees stood the imposing church, its ancient bell tower rising ominously into the slate-grey heavens like an accusing finger pointed at God himself. From within its shadowed heights hung the massive iron bell, a weathered relic of an age long past, its surface etched with the patina of countless seasons. It had rung three times this week already, each hollow, resonant peal marking the passing of another soul claimed by the merciless plague that had wrapped its deadly fingers around their once-peaceful town.

Madeline huddled against the piercing cold, clutching her threadbare wool shawl more tightly around her thin shoulders, though the worn fabric offered little protection against winter's cruel bite. The market square, usually a bustling hub of activity even in the coldest months, stood nearly deserted, its wooden stalls abandoned save for a handful of desperate souls who still dared to sell what meagre goods they had – withered potatoes and stale bread that in better times would have been fed to livestock. The few people who ventured out moved with quick, purposeful steps, their heads bowed against both the wind and their neighbours' gazes, as if the plague might strike them down should they linger too long in one place or meet another's eyes.

She found her gaze drawn inexorably towards the church, and another violent shiver wracked her frame, one born not entirely of cold. The bell loomed large in the collective consciousness of the townspeople, its toll now as dreaded as the telltale signs of the disease itself. Where once it had rung joyously for weddings, christenings, and celebrations, it now served only as death's herald, marking each soul's departure from this mortal plane.

With trembling fingers numbed by cold, she adjusted her grip on the woven basket cradled in her arms, its meagre contents – a few withered vegetables and a half-loaf of bread – barely enough to sustain her mother and herself through another day. She stopped at the nearest stall, picking through a pile of half-rotten turnips with careful deliberation, trying not to wince as the vendor – a gaunt man with hollow cheeks and suspicious eyes – watched her every move with hawk-like intensity, as if expecting her to steal his rotting wares.

"Five pence," he said with a growl, his voice rough from disuse.

"That's too much," Madeline murmured, knowing even as she spoke that arguing was futile. "Surely not for these."

"Then go without," he snapped, pulling the turnips closer to his side of the stall. "There are others who'll pay."

Madeline bit back the sharp retort that rose to her lips. She could not afford to waste her precious breath or energy on pointless arguments, not when her mother needed her strength. Instead, she placed a single copper coin on the stall's weathered surface, knowing full well it wasn't enough, but too weary to care about the proprieties that had governed their lives before the plague. The vendor grumbled but relented, his bony fingers snatching up the coin before tossing a single turnip into her basket with obvious reluctance.

"Best hurry home, girl," he muttered, his voice softening almost imperceptibly. "Strange days these are, strange days indeed."

Madeline turned away quickly, the icy air burning her lungs as she quickened her pace. As she rounded the corner where Market Street gave way to the Hill Road, the imposing silhouette of the Hale estate came into view, its grand stone walls and elegant windows stark against the snow-covered hills beyond. In all her nineteen years, she had never set foot inside those walls, nor did she expect to. The Hale family were aristocrats of the old blood, their wealth and influence as far removed from her own humble existence as the stars themselves. Yet even they, with all their riches and fine physicians, were not immune to the plague's indiscriminate touch; whispers circulated through the town of servants falling ill within those very walls, though Edwin Hale – the family's only son and heir – was said to be as hale as his name suggested, untouched by the disease that ravaged those beneath his station.

"Madeline! Madeline, wait!"

The desperate voice shattered her reverie, and she turned to see Mary, her neighbour's youngest daughter, running towards her through the swirling snow. The girl's face was flushed from exertion, her breath forming rapid puffs of white in the frigid air as she stumbled to a stop.

"It's your mother," Mary panted, clutching a stitch in her side. "She's worse. Much worse than this morning."

Madeline's heart plummeted to her feet, leaving an icy void in her chest that had nothing to do with the winter air. Without another word, she broke into a run, clutching the basket tightly to her chest as her feet carried her automatically through the familiar streets towards home. The world blurred around her – houses, trees, and startled faces melding into a singular impression of grey and white as she ran. Finally, she reached the small cottage she called home, its crooked chimney releasing thin wisps of smoke into the leaden sky. Inside, the air hung heavy with the unmistakable smell of illness – a cloying mixture of sweat, herbs meant to ward off the plague, and something else, something darker that spoke of approaching death.

Her mother lay on the narrow bed beneath the window, her frail body shivering beneath a pile of carefully mended quilts. Madeline knelt beside her, setting the basket down with trembling hands and reaching for her mother's fingers, which felt like ice beneath her touch.

"Mother," she whispered, her voice catching in her throat.

Her mother's eyes fluttered open, once-bright blue irises now glassy and unfocused in her pale face. "Madeline... I heard it again this morning. The bell."

Madeline's breath hitched painfully in her chest. "Hush now, don't speak of it. You need to rest, to save your strength."

But her mother's grip tightened with surprising strength, her voice emerging as little more than a rasp. "Two souls claimed before noon. Each time it rings, I wonder... will the next toll be for me? The plague shows no mercy, does it?"

Madeline shook her head fiercely, tears burning in her eyes though she fought to hold them back. "No, Mother. You're going to recover. You must. I won't let it take you too."

Her mother's gaze softened, though her breathing remained laboured and shallow. "You've always been such a stubborn girl... so strong, just like your father was. Promise me you'll stay that way. When the bell does toll for me..."

"Mother, please, I can't..."

"Promise me, Madeline. Promise me you'll go on."

"I promise," Madeline choked out, her voice barely audible.

The door creaked open on protesting hinges, and Madeline turned to see Mary standing there, wringing her hands in her apron. "I'll fetch the doctor," she offered, though they both knew it was futile. The plague claimed its victims quickly and with cruel certainty; the doctors, for all their learned airs and expensive remedies, could do little but watch and offer empty words of comfort.

As Mary's footsteps faded into the distance, Madeline sat back on her heels, staring at the fire crackling weakly in the hearth, its meagre warmth barely reaching the bed where her mother lay. Outside, the wind howled louder, and somewhere in the distance, the dreaded sound of the bell began to ring again, its deep voice cutting through the winter air with terrible clarity.

Madeline froze, her entire body going rigid as each chime echoed through her bones, filling the tiny room with an oppressive weight that seemed to press the very breath from her lungs. She turned to her mother, whose eyes had drifted closed again, her breathing growing more laboured with each passing moment.

The bell tolled once. Twice. A third time.

"Someone else," her mother whispered, her voice now barely a thread of sound. "The plague takes us all in the end, my dear. Rich or poor, young or old... we all dance to death's tune sooner or later..." Her words trailed off as she slipped into an uneasy sleep, her breathing growing more ragged.

The fire flickered, casting long shadows across the room as the short winter day began to fade. Madeline bowed her head, listening to her mother's increasingly desperate struggle for breath. As darkness fell, the terrible rattling in her mother's chest grew worse, until finally, in the deepest part of the night, it ceased altogether. Madeline sat with tears streaming down her face, knowing that somewhere in the town, a bell-ringer slept, unaware that tomorrow he would need to toll the bell once more.

The fire had burned down to embers, leaving only ghost-light to illuminate her mother's still form. Madeline reached out with trembling fingers to brush a strand of grey-streaked hair from her mother's forehead, her skin already growing cold despite the quilts piled atop her. In the distance, an early-rising rooster crowed, heralding another dawn in Ryehaven – another day of watching, waiting, and counting the toll of the bell.

Chapter Two

Madeline remained motionless by her mother's bed for what felt like an eternity, her tears slowly drying in tracks upon her cheeks as the cold stillness of the room settled around her like a shroud. The remembered echo of the bell's mournful toll lingered persistently in her ears, each phantom ring a cruel reminder of her mother's passing. Beyond the cottage walls, the winter storm continued its relentless assault, great drifts of snow building steadily against the frost-etched windowpanes, muffling the world beyond until it seemed as though she and her grief existed in perfect isolation.

The cottage creaked and groaned under the storm's barrage, its ancient timbers protesting against the wind's fury. Yet even these familiar sounds felt hollow now, empty of the warmth and life her mother's presence had brought to their humble home. The herbs that hung from the rafters – rosemary, thyme, and other remedies that had proved useless against the plague – swayed gently in the draft, their dried leaves rustling like whispered prayers.

When she finally forced herself to rise, her limbs were stiff from hours of immobility, her heart as heavy as lead within her chest. The practical matters that followed death pressed upon her mind with crushing weight – she knew what came next, what always came next in this dance of mortality that had become all too familiar in Ryehaven. Death, even in a town brought to its knees by plague, demanded its rituals and observances. She would need to prepare her mother's body for burial, though the mere thought of handling the cold, lifeless form that had so recently held her mother's vibrant spirit made her stomach churn with desperate revulsion.

A sharp, insistent knock at the door interrupted her grim contemplation, the sound startlingly loud in the hushed atmosphere of the death chamber. Madeline wiped roughly at her tear-stained face with trembling hands, trying to compose herself as she crossed the worn floorboards. The door creaked protestingly as she opened it just wide enough to peer out into the storm-wracked night.

Edwin Hale stood on her doorstep, and the sight of him struck her momentarily speechless.

For several heartbeats, she could only stare in mute astonishment, her mind struggling to reconcile the image of the tall, impeccably dressed nobleman before her with the stark reality of her grief-shadowed home. He cut an imposing figure in his heavy wool coat of finest quality, the shoulders dusted with fresh snow that sparkled in the dim light spilling from her doorway. His dark hair, usually so meticulously groomed, was tousled by the wind and flecked with white, lending him an unusually human aspect. But it was his eyes – pale blue and startlingly intense – that captured and held her attention, piercing through her with an intensity that made her chest tighten uncomfortably.

"Miss Madeline," he said, his voice carrying clearly despite its low, measured tone. "I'm sorry for your loss."

Her throat constricted painfully around unspoken words. Of course, thanks to Mary's astute observation, the entire town would know by now; death was the one visitor that never arrived without herald in these plague-ridden days. With mechanical movements, she opened the door wider, letting the bitter wind rush past her into the cottage as she gestured for him to enter.

"Mr Hale," she managed to murmur, stepping aside to allow him passage. "I wasn't expecting visitors – especially at this hour."

"I must apologise for the untimely intrusion," he said as he crossed her threshold, his polished boots leaving dark, wet prints on the worn wooden floor – a stark reminder of the vast gulf between their social stations. "But I felt compelled to offer my condolences in person. I know all too well what it means to lose someone dear to this cursed plague."

Madeline blinked rapidly, caught off guard by the unmistakable sincerity that resonated in his tone. In truth, she knew precious little about Edwin Hale, beyond the oft-whispered tales of his family's considerable wealth and his own peculiarly reclusive nature. The townspeople spoke of him as something of an oddity among the nobility – a young lord who spent more time surrounded by dusty tomes in his library than hosting lavish gatherings, a man who seemed to prefer quiet contemplation to the grand social obligations his station demanded.

"You've shown great kindness in coming," she said quietly, pushing the heavy door closed against the howling storm. "But there's nothing to be done now. My mother..." Her voice cracked treacherously. "She's gone from this world."

Edwin nodded solemnly, his keen gaze sweeping across the humble room with neither judgment nor pity. The dying firelight caught and held in his features, highlighting the aristocratic lines of his jaw and the shadow of evening stubble that softened his usually pristine appearance. "If you find yourself in need of anything – a proper coffin, arrangements for the burial, assistance with the parish – please don't hesitate to ask. My family maintains certain connections that might prove useful in expediting matters."

Madeline hesitated, feeling pride and desperate necessity wage war within her breast. The stark reality of her situation was impossible to ignore – she had no funds for a proper burial, let alone a coffin worthy of her mother's memory. Yet the thought of accepting charity from a man of Edwin's station felt somehow precarious, as though stepping onto ice of uncertain thickness.

"That's very generous of you," she said carefully, weighing each word. "But I wouldn't wish to impose upon your family's goodwill."

"I assure you, it's no imposition whatsoever," Edwin replied, his expression softening almost imperceptibly. "The dead deserve to be laid to rest with dignity, Miss Madeline. Especially in times as dark as these, when proper ceremony so often falls victim to necessity."

His words stirred something unexpected within her – a tiny flicker of warmth amidst the pervasive cold of her grief. She studied his face intently, searching for any hint of condescension or hidden motive in his offer, but found only genuine concern in his steady gaze. Instead of the haughty nobleman she might have expected, she saw a man who, despite his elevated status, seemed to carry the burden of their town's suffering upon his own shoulders.

"Thank you," she said quietly, the words feeling insufficient yet deeply meant. "I... I will accept your help, with gratitude."

A ghost of a smile touched his lips, transforming his serious countenance. "I'm glad to hear it. I'll send word to the carpenter this very evening, before the storm worsens."

As Edwin turned towards the door, preparing to depart, a question that had been building in her mind suddenly burst forth. "Why?" she asked, her voice barely rising above a whisper. "Why would you do this? You don't even know me."

He paused with one gloved hand resting on the doorknob, turning back to regard her with an expression she couldn't quite decipher. "Because I have seen far too much suffering in recent months to stand idly by when I have the means to ease another's burden, even slightly. No one should have to face the darkness of these times alone."

Before she could formulate a response, he had stepped out into the swirling snow, pulling the door firmly shut behind him. Madeline stood rooted to the spot, staring at the space where he had stood, her heart thundering an unusual rhythm in her chest.

For a brief moment, the storm beyond her walls seemed to lose some of its fury, the shadows that lurked in the corners of her home retreating ever so slightly. She made her way back to her mother's bedside, the fire crackling softly in the hearth as if in quiet approval. Though her grief remained as deep and raw as ever, Edwin's unexpected kindness had kindled something within her – a small, fragile light that pushed back against the encompassing darkness, suggesting that perhaps she wasn't as alone as she had feared.

Chapter Three

The morning dawned as bleakly as Madeline's spirits, the fierce storm having finally exhausted itself in the deepest hours before dawn. A thick blanket of pristine snow lay heavy across the town's rooftops, its tremendous weight causing ancient timber beams to creak and groan, while bare tree branches bowed reverently beneath their white burden. The usual cacophony of town life – the clatter of cart wheels, the shouts of vendors, the laughter of children – was muffled to near silence, as if Ryehaven itself mourned alongside her.

For Madeline, the day began with the most difficult task she had ever faced: preparing her mother's earthly remains for their final journey. The knowledge of what must be done sat like lead in her stomach, yet she knew she could not delay. Death waited for no one, especially not in these plague-riddled times.

She worked in profound silence, broken only by the occasional crackle of the freshly-stoked fire and her own shuddering breaths. Her hands trembled uncontrollably as she dipped a clean cloth into the basin of warmed water, the familiar scent of lavender rising from its surface – the last of her mother's precious soap, saved for special occasions that would never come. With infinite tenderness, she washed her mother's face, memorising every line and contour that time and hardship had etched there. Each stroke of the comb through her mother's silver-streaked hair brought fresh tears to her eyes, but Madeline forced them back, channelling her grief into the methodical movements of her hands. This final act of devotion was as much a part of life now as the dreaded tolling of the church bell, as inevitable as the changing of seasons.

When at last she had completed her solemn duty, Madeline carefully draped her mother's body in the patchwork quilt that had warmed the bed through countless winter nights. Each square of fabric held a memory: here, a scrap from her first dress; there, a piece of her father's favourite shirt; and in the centre, a fragment of her mother's wedding dress, carefully preserved through the years. She stepped back, her chest constricting painfully at the sight before her. This still form bore little resemblance to the vibrant woman who had hummed old folk songs while tending their small garden, who had spent countless evenings teaching Madeline to read and sew by precious candlelight, who had somehow managed to keep hope alive even as the plague tightened its grip on their town.

The sharp rap of knuckles against wood startled her from her contemplation. Wiping her hands mechanically on her worn apron, she crossed to the door and opened it to find two men standing in the crisp morning air, their exhalations forming dense clouds that hung between them like unspoken words. The first she recognised as Thomas Fletcher, the town carpenter, his weather-beaten features softened by an expression of genuine sympathy. His normally ruddy complexion had paled somewhat, whether from the cold or the grim nature of his errand, she couldn't say. Beside him stood a young man she didn't know, though his fine wool coat and meticulously polished boots marked him unmistakably as a servant from the Hale estate. His bearing was rigid, formal, yet his eyes held a glimmer of compassion when they met hers.

"Miss Madeline," the carpenter said softly, removing his worn cap with rough hands that spoke of decades of working with wood. "We've brought what was requested."

Madeline stepped aside wordlessly, her throat too constricted to form a proper response. The men manoeuvred their burden through the narrow doorway – a coffin crafted from pine, simple in design but beautifully made, its wood smooth and free from knots. It was far more than she could have hoped for, far more than most plague victims received in these desperate times. She watched in silence as they placed it with infinite care beside her mother's bed, their movements careful and respectful.

"The master sends his regards," the footman announced with a slight bow, his cultured accent marking him as clearly as his fine clothing. "He wishes to know if you'll require any additional assistance with the burial arrangements."

Madeline shook her head, struggling to find her voice. "Please convey my deepest gratitude to Mr Hale for his extraordinary generosity. I believe I can manage the rest."

The footman nodded solemnly, and both men took their leave, the door remaining slightly ajar in their wake. For several long moments, Madeline stood motionless in the cold draft that whispered through the gap, her gaze fixed on the empty street beyond. Then, drawing a deep, steadying breath, she closed the door firmly and turned to face the task that lay before her.

***

The funeral was arranged with the swift efficiency that the plague had made necessary. There was little room for elaborate ceremony now, and the town gravedigger's services were in constant demand. That afternoon, a modest procession wound its way through the snow-covered streets towards the churchyard: Madeline at its head, followed by Mary, whose tears fell freely, and a small handful of neighbours who had known her mother in happier times, before the plague had turned friendship into a potentially deadly risk.

The priest stood at the edge of the freshly-dug grave, his voice carrying low and solemn across the winter air as he read passages from the Book of Common Prayer. Delicate snowflakes drifted down from the leaden sky, dusting the mourners' shoulders and cloaks, muffling their footsteps and soft murmurs of prayer. Madeline stood slightly apart from the others, her fingers twisted tightly in the threadbare hem of her shawl as she watched four men carefully lower her mother's coffin into the waiting earth. The ropes creaked softly with their burden, and each thud of soil upon wood resonated through her very bones.

When the brief service concluded, the other mourners departed with unseemly haste, eager to escape both the biting cold and the omnipresent spectre of contagion. Only Madeline remained, rooted to the spot, her eyes fixed upon the mound of freshly turned earth that now marked her mother's final resting place. The newly carved wooden marker seemed stark and inadequate to commemorate a life so fully lived, so deeply loved.

"You shouldn't linger here too long," a familiar voice spoke softly behind her. "The cold can be as deadly as any plague."

She turned to find Edwin Hale standing a respectful distance away, his tall figure cut imposingly against the winter landscape. His fine coat was pulled tight against the persistent wind, and a few errant snowflakes had settled in his dark hair.

"I didn't expect to see you here," she said, unable to mask her surprise at his presence.

He stepped closer, his boots crunching rhythmically through the fresh snow. "I came to pay my respects," he said simply. "Your mother was known throughout the town for her kindness. Even my own mother spoke highly of her, before..." He trailed off, leaving the thought unfinished.

Madeline nodded, her throat constricting around unshed tears. "She was special," she managed. "She... she always spoke well of your family. She said the Hales were different from other nobles, that you understood the value of kindness. I never truly believed her until now."

A faint smile touched Edwin's lips, though his eyes remained serious, even troubled. "The world shows us enough cruelty without us adding to it needlessly. If my family's name and resources can bring any measure of comfort in these dark times, then I'm grateful to provide it."

They stood in companionable silence for several long moments, the winter wind whistling softly through the forest of gravestones that surrounded them. Madeline found herself drawing an unexpected warmth from Edwin's presence, a sense of security and solace she hadn't experienced since the plague first reached their town. But the feeling was fleeting, chased away by the sharp awareness of the vast social chasm that separated them – a distance far greater than the few feet of snow-covered ground between where they stood.

"Thank you," she said finally, the words seeming wholly inadequate. "For everything you've done. I don't know how I could ever hope to repay such kindness."

"There's no need for repayment," he said gently, his eyes meeting hers with surprising warmth. "I only hope you'll allow me to offer further assistance should the need arise."

She hesitated for a moment before nodding slowly. "You've shown me more kindness than I could have imagined possible in these times."

With a slight, formal bow that somehow managed to convey genuine respect rather than mere courtesy, Edwin turned and walked away. His dark figure soon disappeared among the silent gravestones, leaving Madeline alone with her thoughts and the endless white of the snow-covered churchyard.

As she finally turned her steps towards home – towards the empty cottage that would never again ring with her mother's laughter – the church bell began to toll once more, its mournful voice echoing across the frozen landscape. She stopped in her tracks, her heart thundering against her ribs as the sound rolled over her like a physical wave. Another life claimed by the merciless plague, another soul departed from this world of suffering.

She thought of Edwin, of his quiet strength and unexpected compassion, of the way his presence had momentarily lightened the crushing weight of her grief. The bell tolled again, its deep voice carrying across the snow-covered town, and Madeline found herself whispering a desperate prayer into the winter wind – a plea that this terrible disease would spare him, that she would never have to hear the dreaded bell toll for Edwin Hale.

Chapter Four

The days that followed her mother's passing drifted by like leaves caught in an autumn wind, each one blending seamlessly into the next until Madeline could scarcely tell them apart. The cottage, once alive with her mother's gentle humming and the soft rustling of her skirts against the floorboards, now echoed with an emptiness that seemed to grow more profound with each passing hour. The familiar creaks of the old wooden beams and the whisper of wind through the thatched roof only served to emphasise the deafening silence where her mother's voice should have been.

Madeline threw herself into the daily tasks that had once seemed mere routines but now became lifelines to sanity. Each morning, she forced herself to trudge through the knee-deep snow to the well, her breath forming delicate clouds in the frigid air as she struggled with the frozen rope and creaking mechanism. The walk back was always harder, the water sloshing dangerously in her bucket, threatening to spill and freeze into treacherous patches on the well-worn path. Inside, she devoted hours to maintaining the meagre fire in the hearth, carefully rationing their dwindling supply of wood, positioning each log just so to extract the maximum warmth from the flames that seemed to grow smaller with each passing day. Yet despite her efforts, the cold seemed to seep through every crack and crevice, as if the winter itself was trying to claim the space her mother had left behind.

The oppressive solitude wrapped around her like a heavy cloak, making even the simplest tasks feel monumental. The cottage's familiar corners, where she had once found comfort, now seemed to loom over her, filled with shadows that stirred memories she wasn't ready to face. Every object held an echo of her mother – the worn chair where she had sat to mend their clothes, the cup she had used for her morning tea, the blanket she had wrapped around herself in her final days. The weight of absence pressed down on Madeline with the same inexorable force as the iron-grey winter sky that hung low over the town.

Since the day they had laid her mother to rest in the frozen ground, the bell had rung out several times again across the frost-covered valley. Each dolorous note sent icy tendrils of fear down Madeline's spine, the sound carrying with it an almost physical presence that seemed to wrap around her throat and squeeze. In the town, people spoke of the bell's toll in whispers, their voices dropping instinctively as if merely discussing it might somehow summon death to their own doorstep. The conversations would cease abruptly whenever she passed by, but their eyes followed her, filled with a mixture of pity and fear, as if her grief might somehow be contagious. Though Madeline tried to push their whispered conversations from her mind, their words seemed to follow her home each evening, clinging to her thoughts like burrs on a woollen skirt.

As the sun began to sink several evenings after the burial, casting long shadows across the snow-covered ground, an unexpected knock shattered the silence of the cottage. The sound was so sudden, so out of place in the stillness that had become her constant companion, that Madeline nearly dropped the pot she had been scrubbing. She stood frozen, cloth still in hand, her heart thundering in her chest. Visitors had become rare treasures – or dangerous omens – since the plague had first appeared in their town. Few dared to risk crossing another's threshold, each home having become both a sanctuary and a potential prison.

When she finally gathered the courage to open the door, the sight of Edwin standing on her doorstep sent a flutter of surprise through her chest that she couldn't quite name. The fading daylight caught in his dark hair, and his broad shoulders were dusted with fresh snow.

"Mr Hale," she managed, his surname feeling oddly formal on her tongue given all that had passed between them. "What brings you to my door at this hour?"

Without ceremony or social niceties, Edwin stepped across her threshold, his boots leaving damp impressions on the wooden planks. His presence seemed to fill the small space, bringing with it a current of cold air and something else – something alive and vital that made the cottage feel less like a tomb. "I've come to see how you're managing," he said, his voice carrying the same quiet authority she remembered. He placed a cloth-wrapped bundle on her small table with careful deliberation. "And I've brought you something."

The sight that greeted Madeline as she unwrapped the cloth made her breath catch in her throat. Fresh bread, its crust still carrying a hint of warmth from the baker's ovens, sat beside a generous wedge of hard cheese and a small clay jar of golden honey. Such provisions had become as precious as gold in recent weeks; the market stalls stood empty more often than not, and what little food was available commanded prices that would have made even the wealthy think twice.

"I cannot accept such generosity," Madeline protested, though her empty stomach clenched traitorously at the sight of the food, reminding her that she had been surviving on little more than thin porridge and hope. The thought of such abundance made her dizzy with want, even as her pride urged her to refuse.

Edwin's response came swift and brooked no argument, his tone carrying the certainty of someone used to having his decisions respected. "You can, and more importantly, you must," he said, fixing her with a steady gaze that seemed to see straight through her protests to the hunger beneath. "I won't stand idly by and watch you waste away in this cold."

Madeline studied his face intently, searching for the telltale signs of pity or obligation that she had grown so accustomed to seeing in others' eyes. But Edwin's expression remained steadfast and clear, his features arranged in lines of simple determination rather than condescension. His presence carried no hint of charity's bitter aftertaste – only a resolute certainty that left her usual defences feeling somehow inadequate.

"Thank you," she whispered finally, the words barely stirring the air between them. It felt insufficient, this simple acknowledgment of his kindness, but anything more seemed to stick in her throat.

Edwin inclined his head in acknowledgment, his eyes moving deliberately around the room, taking in details she would rather he didn't notice. His gaze lingered on the hearth, where the fire struggled against the encroaching cold. "Do you have sufficient firewood?"

Madeline's eyes darted involuntarily to the rapidly diminishing stack of logs beside the fireplace. "It should see me through the next few days," she said, trying to inject more confidence into her voice than she felt.

"I'll have Thomas bring you more tomorrow," he stated, making it sound less like an offer and more like an immutable fact. "You shouldn't have to concern yourself with such matters, not now."

A flash of her old independence flared in her chest at his tone, despite her recognition of the kindness behind it. "I've managed to keep this household running thus far," she said, lifting her chin slightly. "I'm not some helpless child in need of constant minding."

"No one who knows you would ever make that mistake," Edwin replied, and the slight curve of his lips held something warmer than mere amusement. "But even the most capable among us must occasionally admit that strength alone isn't enough to weather every storm."

His words struck home with unexpected force, finding purchase in the carefully maintained walls of her self-reliance. How long had she been fighting? Years of struggling to maintain their modest home, of watching her mother's health slowly fail while trying to preserve their dignity in the face of mounting hardship, of enduring the subtle and not-so-subtle judgments of those who looked down on their circumstances. It all suddenly felt overwhelming, and the prospect of accepting help no longer seemed quite so much like surrender.

"Perhaps you have a point," she conceded, surprising herself with the admission.

Edwin's smile broadened slightly, warming his features. "I'm glad we agree. Now I'll take my leave, before you have time to reconsider your moment of wisdom."

He turned towards the door but paused with

his hand on the latch, looking back at her with an expression she couldn't quite read in the failing light. "Madeline... should you find yourself in need of anything – anything at all – you know where I can be found."

She could only nod, finding herself suddenly unable to trust her voice with the emotions that threatened to overflow.

After his departure, the cottage felt different – not warm, perhaps, but less bitter with cold. Madeline sat in her mother's old chair by the fire, allowing herself to savour each bite of the bread and cheese he had brought, letting the simple flavours fill her mouth and her mind. For the first time since they had lowered her mother into the frozen earth, she felt something stir in her chest that might have been hope, fragile as a sparrow's wing but present nonetheless.

But as she lay in her bed that night, staring into the darkness that pressed against her windows like a living thing, the bell's toll shattered the stillness once more. Its deep, resonant voice seemed to fill the world with its terrible message, each note heavy with the weight of impending loss. Madeline sat bolt upright in her bed, her heart hammering against her ribs as if trying to escape. Her thoughts flew immediately to Edwin – to his kind eyes that crinkled at the corners when he smiled, to the steady timbre of his voice that seemed to ground her even in her darkest moments.

The bell's voice rose again, its second toll rolling across the snow-covered town like a wave of dread. Madeline found herself whispering the same desperate prayer that had become all too familiar recently, her voice barely a breath in the darkness.

"Not him," she pleaded with whatever power might be listening. "Please, God, not him."

Chapter Five

Dawn crept into Madeline's cottage with an unsettling quietude that seemed to press against her. It was the profound silence that only came in the wake of a tremendous snowfall, when the world lay buried beneath a thick white blanket that muffled every sound. As consciousness gradually returned to her, she became aware of the biting cold that had settled into the small space overnight. Her breath escaped in delicate clouds that hung suspended in the grey morning light before dissipating like phantoms. She sat up slowly, her muscles protesting from a night spent tense with worry, and rubbed her arms vigorously in a futile attempt to generate warmth.

With movements made sluggish by the cold, she slipped from beneath her blankets and padded to the hearth. The previous night's fire had dwindled to mere embers, tiny points of orange glowing stubbornly among the ashes. Kneeling before the fireplace, she carefully arranged kindling around the dying coals, coaxing them back to life with gentle breaths until small flames began to dance among the twigs. She drew her worn shawl more tightly around her shoulders, the rough wool offering little comfort against the pervasive chill.

Sleep had proved elusive through the long hours of darkness, her mind refusing to settle. The memory of the bell's sonorous toll echoed in her thoughts, leading her down endless paths of speculation. Who had been claimed this time? Each possibility her mind conjured seemed worse than the last, but inevitably, her thoughts returned to Edwin. Though she had no concrete reason to fear for his safety – he was healthy, well-fed, and lived apart from the most affected areas of the town – anxiety gnawed at her nonetheless. The more she tried to dismiss these concerns as irrational, the more firmly they took root in her consciousness.

As the morning wore on, the confines of the

cottage began to feel oppressive, the walls seeming to close in around her like the pages of a book being shut. Her worried thoughts bounced off the familiar surfaces, multiplying until they threatened to overwhelm her. Finally, despite the bitter cold that waited outside, Madeline could bear the enclosed space no longer. The need to move, to know, to see for herself: they all outweighed her desire for shelter. She pulled on her boots, the leather stiff with cold, and wrapped herself in her heaviest cloak. With practiced movements, she bound her hair beneath a woollen scarf, tucking away every strand that might invite the frost's bite.

The world outside had been transformed overnight into an unfamiliar landscape. The town square, usually alive with activity even in winter, lay silent and strange beneath its new white mantle. The few people who dared to venture out moved like wraiths through the snow, their dark clothes stark against the pristine whiteness, their faces hidden behind scarves and turned away from the wind. Madeline's boots broke through the crystalline surface with each step, the sound seeming unnaturally loud in the hushed atmosphere. She made her way towards the church, its imposing bell tower reaching upward like a dark finger pointing accusingly at the colourless sky. Though she told herself she had come to light a candle in memory of her mother – a proper daughter's duty – she knew the true purpose that drove her feet along this path. She needed to know if Edwin was safe, needed to quiet the fears that had plagued her through the night.

The ancient church door protested her entry with a groan that reverberated through the empty space, making her wince at the disruption of the sacred silence. Within, the air hung thick with the mingled scents of beeswax candles and age-darkened wood, the familiar smell wrapping around her like an embrace from childhood. A scattered few of her fellow townsfolk knelt in the pews, their forms hunched in prayer, their features obscured by layers of winter clothing. Their presence felt both communal and isolating – each lost in their own private supplications to a God who seemed increasingly distant.

She approached the altar with hesitant steps, aware of the echo of each footfall against the stone floor. Her hands shook slightly as she selected a slender candle and touched its wick to one already burning. The small flame flickered to life, adding its light to the constellation of prayers already glowing before the altar.

"Miss Madeline."

The unexpected voice caused her to start, the candle wavering dangerously in her grasp before she steadied it. She turned to find Father Gregory materialising from the shadows near the vestry. The priest had always reminded her of the church itself – tall, severe, and bearing the weight of centuries. His deep-set eyes seemed to hold both the authority of his office and the deep weariness of one who had witnessed too much suffering.

"Father," she acknowledged, dipping her head respectfully.

His lined face softened almost imperceptibly. "Your mother's passing grieved us all," he said, his resonant voice carrying the practiced gravity of one who had spoken such words too often of late. "She was a woman of rare virtue."

"You're kind to say so," Madeline responded softly, the words feeling inadequate against her loss.

The priest's penetrating gaze studied her face with an intensity that made her want to look away. "The night was unkind," he said, his voice dropping to little more than a whisper. "Have you heard who was taken?"

Madeline's heart quickened its pace. "No, Father," she admitted, forcing herself to meet his eyes.

A shadow passed across Father Gregory's weathered features, and his eyes lifted briefly towards the bell tower looming above them. When he spoke again, his voice carried a weight that seemed to press the words into the very stones beneath their feet. "Young Jonas Weaver was called to God's embrace."

The news struck Madeline like a physical blow. Jonas, with his unruly red hair and gap-toothed grin, had run laughing through the town square only weeks ago. Jonas, who had proudly shown her the tiny iron horse his father had helped him forge, his small hands still bearing the smudges of the smithy. The relief that flooded through her – relief that Edwin was safe – brought with it a wave of shame so intense she had to close her eyes against it.

"How did it happen?" she asked, though the question was mere formality. They all knew the answer too well by now.

"The plague shows no more mercy to the young than to the old," Father Gregory replied, his words hanging heavy in the space between them.

The silence that descended was profound, broken only by the whisper of wind around the eaves and the occasional crackle of candle flames. Madeline found herself wondering how many more times the bell would toll before the winter's end, how many more families would be torn apart by this invisible enemy that stalked their streets.

The creak of the church door interrupted her dark musings, and she turned automatically towards the sound. Edwin stood in the doorway, snowflakes melting on his broad shoulders, his presence somehow making the vast church seem smaller. The sight of him, solid and alive, sent a wave of relief through her so powerful it made her knees weak.

"Mr Hale," Father Gregory acknowledged with a slight inclination of his head. "What brings you to God's house this morning?"

"I've come to offer prayers for the departed," Edwin replied, but his eyes were fixed on Madeline, speaking a different truth entirely.

Father Gregory's eyebrow rose slightly at this, but he made no comment, merely nodding once more before withdrawing into the shadows of his domain, his soft footsteps fading into the depths of the church.

Madeline found herself moving towards Edwin before she had made a conscious decision to do so, drawn by an invisible force she couldn't name. "You're safe," she uttered, the words escaping unbidden, hanging in the air between them like a confession.

A gentle smile touched his lips, softening the strong lines of his face. "Did you expect otherwise?" he asked, but there was no mockery in his tone. His hand found her arm, the touch warm even through the layers of her clothing. "I told you before, Madeline – you needn't spend your days worrying about my welfare."

But she did worry, and she knew she would continue to do so, regardless of his assurances. The thought of him being taken by the plague, of his name being whispered in hushed tones by the townspeople, of having to light a candle in his memory – it was more than she could bear to contemplate. The intensity of her concern for him should have frightened her, but somehow it felt as natural as breathing.

"I'm glad to see you here," she said quietly, her words carrying more meaning than their simple surface would suggest.

The warmth in his eyes deepened, and Madeline felt colour rise to her cheeks despite the chapel's chill. She lowered her gaze, suddenly aware of how close they stood, of the impropriety of such intimacy in a house of God.

"Come," Edwin said, gesturing towards the door with a slight inclination of his head. "Allow me to escort you home."

She hesitated for a moment, glancing back at the candle she had lit, watching its flame dance among the others. Then she nodded, accepting both his offer and the implicit promise of his company. Together they stepped out into the snow-filled morning, their breath mingling in white clouds before them. As they walked the familiar path to her cottage, Edwin spoke of inconsequential matters – the unusual severity of the winter, a volume of poetry he'd recently finished reading, the ongoing repairs to the manor's east wing. His voice wrapped around her like a warm cloak, and she found the tension gradually easing from her shoulders, her steps falling naturally in rhythm with his. In his presence, even the oppressive silence of the snow-buried town seemed less threatening, as if his very existence somehow held the darkness at bay.

Chapter Six

Time moved strangely in Ryehaven that winter, the days bleeding into weeks with the inexorable flow of a frozen river. Snow continued to accumulate along the town's narrow streets, transforming familiar pathways into treacherous mazes of white and shadow. The drifts grew so high that in some places they reached the lower windows of the cottages, creating smooth white walls that seemed to glow in the weak winter light. Through it all, the plague maintained its merciless grip on the town, claiming lives with a terrible regularity that became almost routine. The toll of the bell had become as much a part of daily life as sunrise and sunset, its deep, resonant voice speaking of fresh losses almost every day. Each ring sent ripples of fear through the community, leaving behind a wake of grief that seemed to freeze in the air like the crystalline patterns on the windowpanes.

Yet even in the midst of such darkness, Madeline found herself nurturing a fragile seed of hope, protecting it as carefully as she tended the embers in her hearth. This tentative optimism had taken root largely due to Edwin Hale's steady presence in her life. True to his word, he had become a regular visitor to her cottage, arriving with an unfailing reliability that gave structure to her days. Each visit brought not only practical necessities – food, firewood, news from the town – but also something far more precious: the warmth of human connection in a world grown cold with isolation.

Their early interactions had been strained with the discomfort of social convention, each word measured against the yardstick of class distinction. Every gesture, every conversation seemed shadowed by the unspoken reality of their different stations in life. Madeline had found herself constantly aware of the fine quality of his clothes, the educated accent in his speech, the thousand small signs that marked him as belonging to a world far removed from her own. Yet as the weeks passed, these barriers began to erode like snow banks in a subtle thaw, giving way to something more natural and unguarded.

The transformation in their relationship revealed itself most clearly one evening as they sat before her modest hearth, the fire casting dancing shadows across the rough-hewn walls. Edwin had arrived carrying a leather-bound volume of poetry, its gilt edges catching the firelight like captured sunshine. Despite Madeline's initial surprise, he had insisted on sharing some verses, throwing himself into the task with an enthusiasm that bordered on the ridiculous.

"And lo!" he proclaimed, one hand pressed dramatically to his chest while the other held the book aloft, "the fair maiden's heart was rent asunder, for her beloved had been dragged to the ocean's depths by a kraken of most tremendous proportions! Its tentacles, vast as ancient oaks, wrapped round his vessel like the fingers of fate itself!"

The spectacle was so absurd, so completely at odds with Edwin's usual dignified demeanour that Madeline found herself overcome with unexpected mirth. Laughter bubbled up from some long-dormant place within her, and though she tried to contain it behind her hand, the sound escaped anyway, bright and genuine. It was the first time she had laughed since her mother's passing, and the realisation brought with it a mixture of joy and guilt that made her chest ache.

"I believe I've discovered my true calling," Edwin declared, snapping the book shut with an exaggerated flourish. "Perhaps I should abandon my responsibilities and join the next travelling theatre company that passes through." His eyes, however, were fixed on her face, warm with satisfaction at having achieved his obvious goal.

The laughter subsided, but the warmth it had kindled remained, spreading through her chest like honey in hot tea. "Mr Hale, your kindness over these past few weeks... I don't know how I can ever repay such generosity."

"Edwin," he corrected, his voice softening to something intimate and gentle. "Please, call me Edwin. And you owe me nothing, Madeline. Your wellbeing is all the repayment I could wish for."

His gaze held hers across the short distance between their chairs, and suddenly that space seemed charged with possibility, as if the very air had become more alive with meaning. The familiar barriers of class and circumstance that usually stood between them seemed to waver like mirages in summer heat. Madeline felt her cheeks warm, and she quickly looked down at her hands twisted together in her lap.

"I still don't understand," she said, her voice barely above a whisper. "Why have you taken such an interest in my welfare? Surely there are others more deserving of your attention."

Edwin settled back in his chair, the wood creaking softly beneath him. His expression grew thoughtful, the firelight casting subtle shadows across the planes of his face. "More deserving? By what measure? I've watched you face loss and hardship with a grace that many in my circle could never hope to match. Your strength isn't borrowed from wealth or position – it comes from something far more valuable within yourself. How could I not admire such quality of character?"

His words sent a confusing mixture of emotions coursing through her. Pride warred with embarrassment, pleasure with discomfort. She wasn't accustomed to such direct praise, particularly from someone of his standing. It made her feel both seen and exposed, like a flower suddenly thrust into bright sunlight after growing in shade.

"Strength isn't something I chose," she replied, studying the rough fabric of her skirt. "It was simply what circumstances required. When there's no other option but to endure, one endures."

"Perhaps," Edwin said, his tone contemplative. "But the manner in which one endures – that's where true character reveals itself. And I find myself..." he paused, choosing his words with careful deliberation, "increasingly drawn to the character I see in you."

The silence that followed was comfortable rather than strained, filled with the gentle sounds of the fire consuming wood and the distant whisper of wind around the eaves. Madeline found her eyes drawn to Edwin's profile, studying the way the firelight played across his features. There was an innate elegance to him, a refinement that spoke of his upbringing, but it was tempered by something else – an accessibility, a thoughtful gentleness that set him apart from others of his class. Yet she could also see the shadows that lingered beneath his surface, like deep water beneath clear ice.

The question formed in her mind before she could stop it. "How is the manor? Has the plague touched your household as well?"

A shadow passed across Edwin's face, and he nodded slowly. "We haven't been spared, no. Several of the servants have fallen ill despite our precautions. We've converted the old nursery wing into a sickroom, trying to keep the illness contained, but..." he trailed off, running a hand through his hair in a rare gesture of frustration. "My father has essentially barricaded himself in his study, convinced that if he avoids all contact with others, he'll somehow remain untouched. He sends servants away if they so much as cough in his presence."

"And your mother?" Madeline asked softly, immediately regretting the question when she saw pain flash across his features.

"She passed last spring," he said, his voice growing quiet. "Before the plague reached

Ryehaven. Consumption took her, though sometimes I wonder if it was grief that did it in the end. She never quite recovered from my brother's death in the war." He paused, then added, "The illness might have been different, but watching her fade away... I suspect you understand the helplessness of it all too well."

"I'm so sorry," Madeline said, her own grief rising to meet his. "I had no idea." She wanted to reach out, to offer some comfort, but propriety held her back. Instead, she added, "It seems death pays little heed to the gates of grand manors or the thresholds of humble cottages."

"Indeed," Edwin agreed, offering her a smile that held both sadness and warmth. "My mother would have understood you, I think. She always said true nobility had nothing to do with birth or wealth. She would have recognised it in you immediately."

The compliment settled around Madeline's shoulders like a cloak, warm but thick with implication. She turned her attention to the fire, watching the flames dance and twist, consuming the wood as surely as time consumed all things. The unspoken possibilities in Edwin's words hung in the air between them, too delicate to acknowledge directly, too significant to ignore completely.

Finally, Edwin rose from his chair, reaching for his coat. "I should return to the manor. The roads become treacherous after dark, and the snow shows no sign of letting up."

Madeline stood as well, following him to the door with steps that felt somehow reluctant, as if her feet had grown heavy with all the things left unsaid. "Thank you for coming," she said, knowing the words were inadequate to express everything she felt. "For the reading, and... well, everything."

He paused at the threshold, turning to face her. The look in his eyes suggested he had more to say, words that hovered just behind his lips, but instead he simply inclined his head. "Goodnight, Madeline."

"Goodnight... Edwin." His given name still felt new on her tongue.

She stood in the doorway, watching his figure grow increasingly indistinct through the falling snow until the darkness and the storm swallowed him completely. Only then did she close the door, leaning against its solid wooden surface as if seeking support for her suddenly unsteady legs. Her heart was racing, though whether from the cold air or something else entirely, she couldn't say.

In the quiet of her cottage, Madeline found herself confronting feelings she had never expected to experience. What she felt for Edwin had grown beyond simple gratitude or even friendship, transforming into something both wonderful and terrifying. But even as these emotions blossomed in her heart, practical concerns sprouted like weeds around them. The distance between their social positions seemed as vast and impossible as the space between stars. What future could there possibly be for a man of his standing and a woman of her circumstances? Surely any hope of more than friendship was nothing but a foolish dream.

And yet, despite all her rational arguments, despite the voice of society that whispered of impossibilities, despite the plague that threatened to tear their world apart, hope continued to grow in her heart like a flower pushing through snow. Perhaps it was foolish, perhaps it would lead only to heartbreak, but she found herself powerless to stop it. Like the candle she had lit in the church, it burned small but steady, refusing to be extinguished by the darkness that surrounded it.

66

Chapter Seven

The snowstorms had persisted relentlessly for days on end, their fierce winds and heavy snowfall isolating the town more completely than ever before. White drifts piled against doorways and windowsills, while icicles formed deadly crystal daggers that hung from every eave. Most people, beaten into submission by the harsh weather, remained steadfastly behind their wooden doors, venturing out only when absolute necessity demanded it. The church bell continued its mournful toll throughout the days and nights, serving as a sombre metronome that marked the plague's relentless march through their community, each resonant strike a reminder of another soul claimed by the merciless disease.

Madeline spent countless hours by her humble hearth, finding what comfort she could in the familiar rituals of domestic life. Her mother's old quilt lay spread across her lap more often than not, its worn fabric telling stories of years past through every carefully mended tear and lovingly repaired seam. When her fingers grew too stiff from fine needlework, she would turn to the precious few books she had managed to salvage from the market square years ago, before everything had changed. The volumes were dog-eared and weather-worn, but they remained treasured possessions, offering escape when reality became too much to bear. Yet no matter how she tried to lose herself in these simple tasks, her thoughts invariably wandered back to Edwin, like a compass needle seeking true north. She hadn't glimpsed even a shadow of him since that evening by the fire, when the warmth between them had seemed to transcend the mere physical heat of the flames. She found herself missing his presence with an intensity that both surprised and frightened her, though she tried her best to push such dangerous feelings aside.

One particularly dreary afternoon, as the ferocious storm finally began to ease into a gentler flurry, the sudden sharp rap of knuckles against her door sent her heart leaping into her throat. Madeline hurried across the worn floorboards, her stockinged feet nearly silent, trying to temper the wild hope that had sprung unbidden in her chest. When she pulled open the heavy wooden door, there stood Edwin himself, his aristocratic features flushed from the biting cold, delicate crystals of snow dusting his dark hair like a crown of diamonds.

"Edwin," she said breathily, unable to prevent the smile that broke across her face like sunlight through storm clouds. The sight of him standing there, real and solid before her, made her realise just how much she had missed him.

"Madeline," he replied, his rich voice carrying a warmth that seemed to chase away the winter chill. Without waiting for a formal invitation, he stepped across her threshold, bringing with him a swirl of snowflakes and the crisp scent of winter air. He shook his heavy coat, sending a shower of melting snow to her floor, and offered her that characteristic lopsided smile that never failed to make her heart flutter traitorously in her chest. "You look well."

"I've had enough food and firewood to keep my body and soul together," she responded, glancing pointedly at him with a mixture of gratitude and gentle reproach. The provisions he had been bringing her had made all the difference between mere survival and something approaching comfort. "Thanks to you."

"I'm glad," he said, his voice softening to a tender timbre. "But I didn't come merely to check on your welfare this time. I thought you might appreciate some company in these isolated days."

Her chest tightened further at his words, hope and anxiety warring within her heart. She gestured towards the chairs by the fire, and he took the one nearest the flames as if it were his rightful place, as if he belonged there in her humble home despite all the social conventions that said otherwise.

"What's the news from the manor?" she asked as she settled herself in the chair opposite him, trying to maintain some semblance of proper distance despite every fibre of her being wanting to draw closer.

"Not much of consequence," Edwin said, leaning forward to rest his elbows on his knees, his patrician features cast in flickering shadows by the firelight. "The servants grow more nervous with each passing day. My father's anxiety has worsened – he's taken to ordering the staff to remain confined to entirely separate wings of the house. As though mere walls and distance could serve as adequate barriers against death's inexorable advance."

Madeline frowned, reading the pain and frustration beneath his carefully controlled expression. "It must be terribly lonely for you there," she observed softly.

"It is," he admitted, the simple confession carrying the weight of countless sleepless nights and silent meals. "But then I come here, to your cottage, and I find it's suddenly so much easier to breathe."

She blinked rapidly, startled by the raw honesty in his words. His gaze held hers steadily, and for a long moment, the air between them seemed charged with an electric current of unspoken emotion, heavy with possibilities that both thrilled and terrified her.

"You make me sound like some sort of miracle cure," she said, attempting to lighten the moment even as she felt warmth flooding her cheeks.

"Perhaps you are," Edwin replied, his tone carrying such serious conviction that it stole her breath away. "You remind me, Madeline, that the world still holds warmth and light, even in the midst of so much darkness and loss."

Madeline looked away, her hands knotting themselves together in her lap as if seeking anchor in a flurry of emotion. She didn't know how to respond to such words, didn't know how to reconcile the desperate hope they kindled with the crushing fear that they could lead only to bitter disappointment. What future could there possibly be for feelings such as these?

"Forgive me," Edwin said, breaking the silence that had fallen between them. "I didn't intend to cause you discomfort with my words."

"You haven't," she assured him quickly, then added more quietly, her voice barely above a whisper: "It's just... difficult for me to comprehend why you would say such things to someone of my station."

"Someone of your station?" he repeated, his brow furrowing in evident displeasure at her words.

"I'm not..." She hesitated, struggling to find words that wouldn't sound like self-pity. "I'm not part of your world, Edwin. I have nothing of value to offer someone like you."

He leaned forward then, his expression filled with such earnest intensity that it nearly took her breath away. "Madeline, I beg you, never think that your worth as a person is somehow tied to your social station. If anything, I find it remarkable how much you've endured with such dignity. You've shown more grace and strength in the face of adversity than anyone I've ever known."

She stared at him, her heart thundering against her ribs like a wild stallion seeking escape. No one had ever spoken to her in such a manner before, as though her daily struggles to survive made her extraordinary rather than invisible, as though her resilience was something to be admired rather than simply expected.

"You're very kind," she managed to say at last, her voice trembling slightly despite her best efforts to steady it.

"I'm merely honest," he corrected firmly, the conviction in his voice leaving no room for doubt.

Their gazes met and held, and for a breathless moment, the world seemed to contract until it contained nothing but the two of them, suspended in this perfect moment of understanding. Madeline felt an almost overwhelming urge to reach out, to bridge the physical distance between them as their words had already bridged their social divide, but she quickly suppressed the impulse. What good could possibly come from allowing herself to hope for something that the rigid structures of their society would never permit to be?

As if sensing her internal struggle, Edwin leaned back in his chair and offered her a gentle smile that somehow managed to convey both understanding and reassurance. "I brought something for you," he said, reaching into the depths of his coat.

From within the fine wool garment, he withdrew a book, its leather cover showing the subtle wear of countless readings but bearing the obvious signs of loving care. Madeline's eyes widened as he extended it towards her, this unexpected treasure making her momentarily forget her earlier reservations.

"It's one of my most beloved volumes," he explained as she carefully took it from his hands. "I thought you might find pleasure in its pages as I have."

She ran her fingers reverently over the cover, her curiosity thoroughly piqued by this tangible piece of Edwin's inner world. "What tale does it tell?"

"It's a story of adventure primarily," Edwin said, a faint, knowing smile playing about his lips. "With perhaps a touch of romance woven through its pages. But at its heart, it's a tale about discovering courage in the face of seemingly insurmountable odds."

Madeline opened the book with infinite care, her fingertips brushing across the pages with something approaching awe. The volume carried the distinctive scent of ink and aged paper, a perfume more precious to her than any expensive fragrance. She felt a wave of gratitude so intense it nearly brought tears to her eyes.

"Thank you," she said, looking up to meet his gaze once more. "This gift means more to me than I could possibly express."

Edwin's expression softened into something that made her heart skip a beat. "You owe me no thanks, Madeline. I only hope it brings you some measure of comfort and joy in these dark times."

They continued talking for what felt like both an eternity and mere moments, their conversation flowing as naturally as a spring stream, warm and intimate despite the winter's chill beyond her walls. When Edwin finally rose to take his leave, Madeline stood at her door and watched his tall figure disappear into the gently falling snow, the book clutched protectively against her chest like a shield against loneliness.

For the first time in what felt like an age, she felt truly, vibrantly alive, as though Edwin's presence had awakened something within her that she hadn't even realised had been sleeping. The snow continued to fall softly outside her window, but somehow, it no longer seemed quite so cold.

Chapter Eight

The book Edwin had given her quickly became more than just a simple story for Madeline – it transformed into a precious lifeline, a bridge across the isolation that threatened to overwhelm her. During the longest hours of the night, when the world beyond her walls felt as barren and desolate as the endless snow-covered fields stretching to the horizon, she would settle herself by the crackling fire and lose herself completely in its pages. The tale within was one of valiant heroes and lovers separated by circumstance and station, and although their world of grand adventures and noble pursuits seemed impossibly far removed from her own humble existence, Madeline found herself drawing strength from their familiar struggles, seeing echoes of her own challenges in their trials.

But it wasn't merely the story itself that held her captivated night after night – it was the constant, warming thought of Edwin that truly made each page precious to her. With every careful turn of the pages, she would imagine him reading these very same words, perhaps sitting in his grand library at the manor, finding depth and meaning in the same passages that touched her heart. It created an intimate connection between them that transcended their physical separation, as though they shared a secret world that existed purely in the realm of imagination, beyond the rigid confines of their socially divided lives.

His visits to her cottage grew more frequent as the weeks passed, and with each one, the bond between them deepened like roots seeking water in fertile soil. He would arrive bearing small gifts that spoke volumes of his thoughtfulness: a freshly baked loaf of bread, a precious vial of golden honey that must have cost more than some earned in a week, or sometimes he would bring nothing at all but his presence and his conversation – the very thing she treasured the most. They would sit together by the dancing flames of her hearth and talk for hours that seemed to pass like minutes, their discussions flowing effortlessly from philosophical debates about the nature of fate to harmless town gossip, from cherished memories of their vastly different childhoods to the dreams they normally kept locked away in the depths of their hearts, too fragile to voice to others.

For Madeline, these precious moments with Edwin served as a blessed reprieve from the plague's shadow that hung over the town. Yet they also brought with them a growing sense of unease that she couldn't quite shake, no matter how she tried. Despite her best efforts, she found it impossible to ignore the way her heart would leap traitorously in her chest at the mere sight of his warm smile, or the tingling warmth that spread through her entire body like wildfire when his hand accidentally brushed against hers. This feeling that had taken root deep within her soul was dangerous, she knew – as dangerous as walking on thin ice over deep water.

One particularly cold evening, as they sat together in the comfortable silence they had come to share, Edwin suddenly leaned forward in his chair, his expression transformed by an intensity she had rarely seen before. "Madeline," he began, his voice carrying something that made her pulse quicken, "there's something I've been meaning to ask you."

Her heart skipped several beats, and she found herself holding her breath. "What is it?" she managed to ask, struggling to keep her voice steady.

"Have you given any serious thought to leaving Ryehaven?" he asked. "The plague has already claimed far too many lives in these parts. I fear it won't relent, and the thought of you remaining here..." He left the sentence unfinished, but his meaning hung heavy in the air between them.

Madeline frowned deeply, her hands twisting in her lap. "Where would someone like me possibly go?" she asked. "This town is my home, Edwin. It's all I've ever known, all I understand of the world."

"There are other places," he pressed earnestly, "places where the plague's shadow hasn't yet fallen. Towns and cities where you could begin anew, where you might find a different path. I could help you secure respectable work, somewhere far safer than here."

She stared at him, her chest constricting painfully as she processed his words. The mere idea of abandoning Ryehaven felt like a physical blow. This town, despite all its hardships and sorrows, was where her mother had lived out her days and drawn her final breath. It was where every memory she possessed had taken root and flourished, where every moment of her life's story had unfolded like pages in a familiar book.

"I cannot leave," she said finally, her voice soft but firm with conviction. "Not now. It just wouldn't feel right."

Edwin's brow furrowed deeply, and she could see him struggling with the urge to argue further, to press his point. But something in her expression must have reached him, for he checked himself. Instead of continuing his plea, he reached across the space between them and took her hand in his, his touch warm and reassuringly steady against her skin.

"Then promise me this at least," he said, his voice thick with emotion. "Promise that you'll allow me to help you through whatever may come. You don't have to face these dark days alone, Madeline."

She looked down at their joined hands, her heart a tempest of conflicting emotions. Gratitude warred with fear, hope battled against practical wisdom. She wanted nothing more than to believe in his words, to trust completely in the strength and sincerity of his kindness. But a persistent voice in the depths of her mind, one that spoke with her mother's practical wisdom, warned her that hope was as fragile as a soap bubble, just as easily shattered by the harsh realities of their world.

"I promise," she whispered at last, the words feeling simultaneously like a victory and a surrender.

A gentle smile touched Edwin's lips, warming his features, and he gave her hand one final, tender squeeze before reluctantly releasing it. They sat together in companionable silence for a long while after that, the fire crackling softly between them like a third presence in the room, offering its own wordless comfort.

As the evening drew to its natural close, Edwin rose from his chair and pulled his heavy wool coat around his shoulders, preparing to face the bitter night air.

Madeline walked him to the door, feeling the immediate bite of winter's chill as she opened it to the darkness beyond.

"Goodnight, Madeline," he said, his voice carrying a warmth that seemed to push back against the cold.

"Goodnight, Edwin," she replied softly, watching as his tall figure was gradually swallowed by the snowy darkness beyond her door.

She closed the heavy wooden door against the night and leaned against it, her heart feeling as though it might burst from the intensity of her conflicting emotions. Never in her life had she felt so powerfully drawn to another soul, nor so painfully aware of the fundamental impossibility of the connection that seemed to be growing between them.

Yet even as doubt gnawed relentlessly at the edges of her mind, she couldn't help but nurture the tender shoot of hope that had begun to bloom within her heart, like a flower pushing through winter soil towards an unseen sun.

***

The next day, the bell's toll shattered the morning's brittle silence. Madeline was outside in the bitter cold, gathering armfuls of firewood from the rapidly dwindling stack behind her cottage, when the deep, resonant sound rang out through the town. She froze in place, some kindling slipping forgotten from her suddenly nerveless fingers.

Her first, immediate thought was of Edwin, and the mere possibility made her blood run colder than the winter air. The toll seemed somehow heavier than usual, more ominous in its sombre resonance. Without conscious thought, she dropped the remaining bundle of wood and began running towards the church, her breath forming desperate clouds in the freezing air as she pushed herself forward.

The town square was unnaturally quiet as she passed through it, the few people she encountered averting their eyes from her desperate passage as though afraid to acknowledge her fear. When she finally reached the church, she found Father Gregory standing solemnly at the base of the bell tower, his aged face carved with lines of sorrow.

"Father," she called out, unable to completely mask the tremor in her voice. "Please, who is it? Who has the bell tolled for?"

The elderly priest turned towards her, his expression wearied by his burden. "The bell tolled for Ruth Baker," he said gently, "the widow who made her home by the old mill."

Relief flooded through Madeline's chest with such force that her knees nearly buckled, followed immediately by a crushing wave of guilt that made her stomach turn. She pressed a trembling hand to her mouth, deeply ashamed of the selfishness of her reaction. Ruth had always been nothing but kind to her, offering warm smiles and gentle words of encouragement whenever their paths had crossed in the town.

"Is there anything I might do to help?" she asked, trying to atone for her momentary selfishness. "Any service I could perform?"

Father Gregory shook his head slowly, his grey hair catching the weak winter sunlight. "The gravedigger has already been summoned to perform his duty. But if you wish to offer a prayer for her soul's peaceful journey, I'm certain it would be most appreciated."

Madeline nodded solemnly and stepped into the church's shadowy interior. The air within was still and cold, the few remaining candles flickering faintly in the dim light that filtered through the high windows. She made her way to the altar and knelt before it, her hands clasped tightly together in desperate prayer.

"Please," she whispered into the sacred silence, her voice breaking with the emotion she could no longer contain. "Keep him safe. I beg you, protect him from harm."

The words hung in the still air of the church like frost crystals, a heartfelt plea directed towards a divine power she wasn't entirely certain she believed in anymore, but one she desperately needed to trust in now.

Chapter Nine

The days that followed Ruth Baker's passing hung over Ryehaven like a shroud, each hour imbued with a suffocating sense of unease that seemed to press down upon every soul in the town. The bell's mournful toll appeared to linger longer in the frozen air with each death, its sorrowful echo reverberating through the narrow streets as a constant, haunting reminder of how terrifyingly fragile life had become in their once-peaceful town. The townsfolk themselves grew increasingly withdrawn, their faces exhausted and wary, as though they feared that merely meeting another's gaze might somehow invite death's attention. Even the precious comfort of Edwin's visits to Madeline's cottage now carried with them a new sense of desperate urgency, as though time itself had become like water running through their fingers, impossible to hold on to no matter how tightly they tried to grasp it.

One particularly bitter afternoon, as the snow fell in thick, relentless curtains outside her window, Edwin arrived at her door with a leather satchel slung across his shoulder. His aristocratic cheeks were flushed crimson from the biting cold, and a rebellious strand of dark hair had fallen across his forehead as he stepped from the winter bleakness into the welcoming warmth of Madeline's humble cottage.

"I hope you won't think me presumptuous," he said, brushing accumulated snow from his expensive coat with gloved hands. "But I brought something I thought we might share."

Madeline felt a small smile touch her lips despite the heaviness in her heart. "You're always welcome here, Edwin. You must know that by now."

He set the well-worn satchel carefully on her rough wooden table and began to unpack its contents with deliberate movements: a freshly baked loaf of bread that still held a hint of warmth, a generous wedge of pale yellow cheese, and most surprisingly, a bottle of deep red wine. To Madeline's eyes, accustomed to the humble portions that had become the norm in these desperate times, it wasn't merely a meal – it was nothing short of a feast.

"Where in heaven's name did you manage to find wine?" she asked, her eyebrows lifting in genuine surprise as she studied the dusty bottle.

"A gift of sorts," Edwin replied with a wry smile that held a hint of mischief. "Or perhaps more accurately, something my father has precious little use for these days. He's barricaded himself so thoroughly in his chambers, I rather doubt he'd notice if half the manor's wine cellar simply vanished into thin air."

Madeline laughed softly at his small act of rebellion, the sound surprising even herself with its genuineness. Edwin looked up at her then, his expression warming like sunshine breaking through storm clouds, and for one precious moment, the room felt lighter than it had in weeks, as though some of the darkness pressing in from outside had retreated just a little.

They settled together by the crackling fire, sharing the simple yet extraordinary meal between them. The wine, though likely modest by Edwin's aristocratic standards, was rich and warming in Madeline's inexperienced opinion, its complex flavour lingering pleasantly on her tongue. She felt an almost dreamlike sense of normalcy wash over her, as though the troubled world beyond her cottage walls had temporarily faded away into nothingness, leaving only the two of them existing together in their small, precious cocoon of warmth and companionship.

As their conversation flowed easily between them, Edwin leaned forward in his chair, his elbows coming to rest on his knees as he gazed into the dancing flames. "Do you ever find yourself wondering what life might have been like, if not for the plague's arrival?" he asked, his voice taking on a contemplative tone.

Madeline tilted her head thoughtfully, considering his question with care. "I suppose I do, from time to time," she admitted. "But those memories feel so terribly distant now, like a half-remembered dream that slips away upon waking. What about you? Do you think often of the time before?"

Edwin's penetrating gaze remained fixed on the fire, his expression growing increasingly pensive. "I find myself wondering about many things these days," he said slowly, as though carefully choosing each word. "About what might have been, had circumstances been different. About what still could be, if fate proves kind. But more than anything else, I find myself wondering why we were spared when so many others weren't."

His words settled over them like a heavy blanket, and Madeline found herself reaching out almost instinctively, her fingers brushing against his hand with butterfly lightness. "Perhaps we were spared for a reason," she said quietly. "Even if we don't yet understand what that reason might be."

Edwin turned his hand beneath hers, clasping her fingers gently but firmly in his warm grip. His touch sent a jolt of something electric and unnamed through her entire body, and when she looked up to meet his gaze, she found herself catching her breath at the raw intensity she saw in his eyes.

"Madeline," he began, his voice dropping to a low, intimate tone that made her heart flutter, "there's something important I need to tell you."

Her heart began pounding so forcefully she felt certain he must be able to hear it. "What is it?" she managed to ask, her voice trembling slightly.

But before he could give voice to whatever confession lay on his lips, the distant, dreaded toll of the church bell shattered their intimate moment like a stone through glass. The sound sent an immediate chill racing down Madeline's spine, and she pulled her hand back from his as though burned, an instinctive reaction born of sudden fear. Edwin's expression darkened visibly, and he stood abruptly from his chair, crossing the small room in long strides to peer out through the frost-covered window.

"Do you think it's someone we know?" she

asked, her voice barely audible even in the sudden silence.

"Most likely," Edwin replied grimly, his shoulders tense. "The town has become too small for it to be otherwise."

Madeline rose from her own chair and joined him at the window, their shoulders nearly touching as they gazed out at the endless curtain of falling snow that muffled the town in its thick white blanket. The bell tolled again, its mournful cry echoing across the snow-laden rooftops like a physical presence.

"I should take my leave," Edwin said suddenly, his tone clipped and formal in a way she hadn't heard from him in weeks.

"You don't have to go," Madeline said quickly, reaching out to grasp his arm, unwilling to let this precious moment end so abruptly.

He turned to face her, his severe expression softening noticeably as their eyes met. "I'll return soon," he promised, his voice gentling. "But I must check on the manor first. If one of the servants has fallen ill..." He trailed off, shaking his head as though to dispel the thought.

Madeline nodded reluctantly, understanding all too well the unspoken weight of his responsibilities to his household. "Please be careful," she said, unable to keep the worry from her voice.

"I will."

He hesitated for a long moment, as though there were words struggling to break free from his lips, but then he turned abruptly and stepped out into the swirling snow. Madeline watched his tall figure gradually disappear into the white darkness, her heart growing heavier with each step he took away from her.

The bell tolled again, its sound somehow more ominous than before, and she closed her eyes tightly, whispering the same desperate prayer she had begun to repeat countless times each day.

"Not him," she murmured into the empty air. "Please, dear God, not him."

***

The night stretched endlessly before her, each hour passing more slowly than the last, like honey dripping from a spoon. Madeline tried desperately to distract herself with the book Edwin had given her, but the familiar words seemed to blur together on the page, their meaning lost in the thick haze of her worried thoughts.

Finally, as the fire dwindled to nothing more than glowing embers in the hearth, she heard a knock at her door. Her heart leapt in her chest, and she rushed to answer it, expecting – hoping – to see Edwin's familiar tall silhouette framed against the night.

Instead, she found her neighbour Mary standing at the threshold, her usually rosy face pale as milk and pinched with obvious worry in the dim light.

"Madeline," Mary said, her voice shaking like a leaf in an autumn wind. "It's Edwin. He's fallen terribly ill."

The words struck Madeline with force, and she found herself gripping the wooden doorframe for support as her knees threatened to buckle beneath her. "What?!" she exclaimed, praying she had somehow misheard.

"They've sent riders to fetch the doctor from the next town," Mary continued, her hands wringing together nervously in front of her worn dress. "But he's burning up with fever already. They don't know yet if it's the plague or something else."

Madeline's mind raced wildly. Without conscious thought, she fearfully reached for her heavy cloak and began pulling on her boots with trembling hands.

"Madeline, you can't possibly go to the manor!" Mary protested, her tone growing frantic. "If it truly is the plague..."

"I have to go," Madeline interrupted firmly, surprising herself with the steel in her voice. "I cannot simply sit here and do nothing while he suffers."

Before Mary could voice any further protests, Madeline stepped out into the biting cold of the winter night, the freezing air stinging her face.

The path to the manor was brutal in the darkness, the snow deep and treacherously uneven beneath her feet, but she pressed forward regardless, her determination to reach Edwin's side far outweighing any fear for her own safety.

As the bell's toll echoed into the vast, indifferent night, Madeline whispered a desperate prayer to the cold, uncaring sky above.

"Please," she said, shivering and almost out of breath, her words forming small clouds in the frozen air. "Just let me reach him in time."

Chapter Ten

The path to the Hale manor proved far more treacherous than Madeline had dared to anticipate, each step a battle against the elements that seemed determined to impede her progress. The freshly fallen snow, beautiful though it might have been under different circumstances, clung persistently to her skirts like grasping fingers, weighing down her every movement. It seeped mercilessly through the worn leather of her boots – boots that had never been intended for such a journey – until she could scarcely feel her feet except for the sharp, biting cold that had settled deep into her bones.

By the time the imposing manor finally came into view through the swirling snow, Madeline's breath came in shallow, ragged gasps that formed dense clouds in the frigid air. Her limbs felt leaden, every movement a conscious effort that required increasingly more of her diminishing strength, but she forced herself forward with grim determination. The grand stone structure loomed against the ink-black winter sky like a creature from a fairy tale, its windows glowing with the warm, faint flicker of candlelight that seemed to beckon her forward. On any other evening, the mere sight of the estate would have filled her with an overwhelming sense of unease – a stark and crushing reminder of the vast social divide that separated her modest life from Edwin's world of privilege and propriety – but tonight, all she could focus on was reaching him, on confirming with her own eyes that he still drew breath.

When she finally reached the wooden doors, ornately carved with the Hale family crest, she gathered what remained of her strength and pounded against them with desperate intensity, her knuckles stinging from the impact. The seconds stretched into what felt like hours before the ancient hinges finally creaked in protest, and the right door swung inward to reveal a frazzled-looking servant, his greying hair dishevelled and his livery slightly askew.

"Miss Madeline?" the man said, his eyes widening with undisguised surprise as he recognised her. The genuine shock in his voice made it clear that her presence was as unexpected as it was improper. "Whatever are you doing here at this ungodly hour? And in such weather?"

"I need to see Edwin," she managed between laboured breaths, her voice carrying all the urgency that had driven her through the storm. "Word reached me that he's fallen ill. Please, I must see him."

The servant hesitated visibly, his features creasing with concern as he glanced furtively over his shoulder, as if expecting the stern reproach of the housekeeper or, worse yet, a member of the Hale family to materialise from the shadows. "He's resting now," he said with careful diplomacy, lowering his voice. "The doctor is attending to him at present."

"Please," Madeline pleaded, allowing her desperate worry to show plainly on her face. "I swear I won't interfere or cause any disturbance. I just need to know with my own eyes that he's all right. I couldn't bear another moment of not knowing."

Something in her voice – perhaps the raw emotion, or maybe just the simple human understanding of love's desperate nature – caused the man's face to soften perceptibly. After another moment's hesitation, he stepped aside with a slight bow, motioning for her to enter. The blessed warmth of the manor enveloped her like a physical embrace as she stepped across the threshold, bringing with it the genteel fragrance of lavender water and wood smoke that seemed to permeate the walls.

"Follow me," the servant instructed in hushed tones, lifting a candlestick from a nearby table and leading her through the dimly lit corridors of the sleeping house.

The manor's interior was every bit as grand as she had imagined in her daydreams, its walls adorned with imposing oil paintings of stern-faced Hale ancestors and its floors covered in thick, intricately patterned rugs that muffled their footsteps. But Madeline barely registered any of it, her mind consumed entirely by thoughts of Edwin and the state in which she might find him.

When they reached the oak door that led to his chambers, the servant paused, turning to face her with an expression of gentle warning. "He may not be conscious," he cautioned her quietly. "The fever has been quite severe."

Madeline nodded her understanding, her throat too tight with emotion to form words, and the man gently pushed open the door, gesturing for her to enter the darkened room.

The chamber was dimly illuminated by a single beeswax candle that flickered on the bedside table, casting dancing shadows across the elegant furnishings. Edwin lay still and silent in the massive canopied bed, his usually handsome face pallid and glistening with a sheen of fever-sweat that caught the wavering light. The doctor – a stout, serious-looking man with a gleaming bald pate – stood vigilant at his bedside, methodically pressing a cool, damp cloth to Edwin's burning forehead.

At the sound of her footsteps on the polished floorboards, the doctor turned sharply, his expression morphing from surprise to clear disapproval at this unexpected intrusion. "Who are you?" he demanded in clipped tones that spoke of his position and authority. "This is most irregular."

"I'm a friend," Madeline said simply, drawing closer to the bed despite the doctor's obvious displeasure. Her eyes never left Edwin's face as she asked, "How severely is he affected? Will he recover?"

The doctor hesitated, his professional demeanour warring visibly with his obvious desire to simply dismiss her from the room. His eyes darted between her face and Edwin's unconscious form before he finally spoke, his voice gruff but not unkind. "He is suffering from a dangerous fever," he admitted reluctantly. "There are concerning similarities to the early stages of the plague, though it's still too soon to make such a grave determination. For now, what he requires most is complete rest and careful attendance."

Moving to the bedside with steps that felt both hesitant and inexorable, Madeline felt her heart constrict painfully at the sight of Edwin looking so utterly defenceless. His breathing was laboured and shallow, his broad chest rising and falling with visible effort beneath the fine linen of his nightshirt. Unable to resist the urge to offer some small comfort, she reached out with trembling fingers to brush a damp strand of his dark hair away from his burning forehead.

"Edwin," she whispered, her voice quavering with the depth of her concern. "I'm here now."

His eyelids fluttered at the sound of her voice, and slowly, with what seemed like tremendous effort, he managed to open them. The usual sharp intelligence and warmth in his eyes was dulled by the fever's grip, but when his gaze finally focused on her face, his cracked lips curved into a weak but genuine smile. "Madeline," he murmured, his voice barely more than a hoarse whisper. "You're actually here. I thought I must be dreaming."

"Of course I'm here," she responded, unable to prevent the tears that sprang to her eyes at the sound of his weakened voice. "How could I stay away when I heard you were ill? You gave me such a fright."

He closed his eyes briefly, as if the simple act of keeping them open required more strength than he could muster. When he spoke again, his voice was threaded with concern despite its weakness. "You shouldn't... you shouldn't have risked coming here. It's not safe. If you were to fall ill as well..."

"Hush now," she admonished him gently, her heart swelling with both love and worry at his typical selflessness. "Don't waste your precious energy worrying about me. You need to focus on getting well."

The doctor cleared his throat pointedly, drawing her attention away from Edwin's face. When she looked up, his expression had softened somewhat, though concern still creased his brow. "If you are determined to remain here, you must exercise extreme caution," he instructed firmly. "Maintain as much distance as possible when not directly attending to his needs, and wash your hands frequently with soap and hot water. This particular illness has proven itself to be remarkably unforgiving in its spread."

"I'll follow your instructions to the letter," Madeline assured him with quiet determination. "I'll do whatever is necessary to help him recover."

The doctor studied her face intently for a long moment, apparently finding something in her expression that satisfied him, for he finally nodded his approval. "Very well," he conceded. "I shall return at first light to check on his condition. Send for me immediately if his fever spikes or his breathing becomes more laboured."

As the doctor gathered his medical bag and various implements, Madeline pulled a delicate rosewood chair closer to the bedside and carefully took Edwin's hand in both of hers. His skin burned against her palm, and his usually strong fingers lay limp and unresponsive in her gentle grasp.

"Why must you always be so stubborn?" he murmured, managing another weak smile despite his obvious exhaustion. "Braving a snowstorm just to sit beside a sick man's bed?"

"I could ask you the same question about your own stubborn nature," she replied, her voice thick with the emotion she struggled to contain. "Always pushing yourself too hard, never admitting when you need rest."

They lapsed into a comfortable silence then, broken only by the mournful howling of the wind beyond the leaded glass windows. Madeline watched attentively as Edwin drifted in and out of consciousness, her heart constricting painfully with every difficult breath he drew.

"You cannot leave me," she whispered fervently when she was certain he had fallen into a deeper sleep, her voice barely audible even to her own ears. "I simply won't allow it. We have too much left to experience together."

As the long hours of the night wore on, she maintained her vigil faithfully by his side, regularly refreshing the cool cloth on his brow and whispering words of comfort and encouragement whenever he stirred. Though fear and uncertainty about what the coming dawn might bring lurked at the edges of her thoughts, she refused to let them take hold.

Edwin had been her beacon of hope during the darkest period of her life, appearing like a guardian angel when she had thought all was lost. Now, as she watched over his fitful sleep and prayed for his recovery, she knew it was her turn to be his light in the darkness, to give him the strength and hope he needed to fight his way back to health.

Chapter Eleven

The night seemed to stretch endlessly before Madeline as she maintained her position faithfully by Edwin's bedside, her smaller hand wrapped protectively around his larger one, watching helplessly as the fever continued its relentless assault on his body. The furious winter wind howled like a savage beast beyond the manor's walls, rattling the windows in their leaded frames, but Madeline's attention never wavered from Edwin's face – so pale now, so unlike its usual healthy vigour, with beads of sweat glistening in the wavering candlelight.

In his fevered sleep, Edwin would occasionally break the chamber's silence with mumbled words that tore at Madeline's heart. Though largely incomprehensible, his utterances carried such profound sorrow that she could barely stand to hear them. Each time, she would lean closer, her movements gentle and precise as she drew a fresh, cool cloth across his burning forehead. "Hush now, Edwin," she would whisper, her voice soft but steady despite her growing fear. "You're not alone. I'm here with you, and I won't leave your side."

The endless hours of night blended together in a haze of worry and exhaustion, and when dawn finally began to paint the eastern sky, it brought with it none of the hope or relief that Madeline had desperately prayed for. The weak winter morning light filtered reluctantly through the heavy velvet curtains, casting long, distorted shadows across the ornate furnishings of the room. Edwin's condition remained frustratingly unchanged, and with each shallow, laboured breath that passed his lips, Madeline felt the vice around her heart tighten further.

The ancient hinges of the chamber door announced the doctor's arrival with a prolonged creak, and Madeline turned to see him entering with his characteristic air of professional gravity. His face, though composed, carried the weight of concern that made her stomach clench with renewed worry. He set his worn leather medical bag down on a nearby table with practiced care and approached the bed, acknowledging her presence with a curt but not unkind nod.

"How has he fared through the night?" he enquired, his tone carefully neutral as he began his morning examination.

"His fever persists without breaking," Madeline reported quietly, unconsciously tightening her grip on Edwin's hand. "And his breathing remains shallow – perhaps more so than before."

The doctor's frown deepened as he placed an experienced hand against Edwin's forehead, his fingers moving to check the pulse at his patient's wrist with methodical precision. After what seemed like an eternity, he stepped back from the bed, his expression carefully schooled to reveal nothing of his thoughts.

"It remains too early to make any definitive pronouncements," he said, maintaining his professional demeanour. "However, we can take some small comfort in the fact that the fever has not worsened over the night. I shall prepare a tincture that should help ease his laboured breathing."

"Will such a remedy be sufficient?" Madeline asked, unable to keep the tremor of fear from her voice. "Will it be enough to save him?"

The doctor hesitated, removing his spectacles to polish them with a pristine handkerchief – a gesture that seemed more about buying time to choose his words carefully than any real need to clean the lenses. Finally, he sighed, his professional façade softening slightly. "That, my dear, depends entirely upon his own strength of constitution – and more importantly, his will to fight this affliction."

Madeline's gaze returned to Edwin's face, her heart sinking deeper in her chest as she took in his vulnerable state. He looked so terribly fragile lying there, so devastatingly unlike the strong, confident man who had captured her heart with his quiet strength and unwavering principles. Yet even as despair threatened to overwhelm her, she felt a spark of determination ignite in her soul. She would not surrender him to this illness without a fight.

"Tell me what needs to be done," she said, her voice taking on a resolute edge that seemed to surprise the doctor. "What can I do to help him?"

"Keep him as comfortable as possible," the doctor instructed, beginning to gather various vials and herbs from his bag. "Continue your efforts to cool his fever, and ensure he takes in fluids whenever he shows signs of consciousness. Beyond these measures, I'm afraid we can do little but wait and pray."

Madeline nodded firmly, her features set with grim determination. She had not braved a snowstorm and defied propriety only to stand idle while Edwin slipped away from her. She would fight for him with every ounce of strength she possessed.

The doctor handed her a small crystal vial containing the promised tincture, providing detailed instructions for its administration before taking his leave. Once alone with Edwin again, Madeline turned her full attention back to him, her hands steady despite the turbulent emotions threatening to overwhelm her. With practiced care, she measured several drops of the tincture into a porcelain cup of fresh water, supporting Edwin's head gently as she encouraged him to drink.

"Come now, Edwin," she whispered, her voice carrying all the strength she wished she could somehow transfer to him. "You must fight this. You're stronger than any fever – I know you are. Don't you dare let it defeat you."

As the hours of daylight slowly passed, Madeline felt her own exhaustion beginning to take its toll on her body. Her eyelids grew increasingly heavy, and her muscles protested painfully from maintaining the same position for so many hours. Yet each time the thought of rest crossed her mind, she banished it immediately with fierce determination. Edwin needed her vigilance now more than ever, and she would not fail him by surrendering to her own weakness.

The manor's servants came and went throughout the day, moving quietly about their duties with admirable discretion. Though they spoke little, their concern for both Edwin and herself was evident in countless small acts of kindness – a steaming bowl of nourishing soup appearing precisely when she needed it most, a thick woollen blanket thoughtfully draped across her shoulders when the fire burned low, fresh linens provided without having to be asked.

As evening approached once more, Edwin stirred slightly in his bed, his eyes fluttering open for the briefest of moments. Madeline leaned forward instantly, hope blazing to life in her chest with an intensity that nearly took her breath away.

"Edwin," she called softly, not daring to raise her voice above a whisper. "Can you hear me? I'm here with you."

His lips moved slightly, though no sound emerged, and his eyes slipped closed again before she could be certain he had truly seen her. Still, small as it was, this sign of life was enough to rekindle the flame of hope in her heart that had begun to flicker dangerously low.

***

The night hours crept by with agonising slowness, the oppressive quiet broken only by the sound of Edwin's laboured breathing and the occasional crackle of the fire. Madeline dozed fitfully in her chair, her exhausted mind plagued by troubling dreams in which the ominous tolling of the bell merged with haunting visions of Edwin slipping away from her reaching hands into an impenetrable darkness.

When she startled awake some time later, the chamber was suffused with the pale, uncertain light of early dawn. Her heart leaped as she noticed Edwin stirring slightly in his bed, his breathing noticeably steadier and deeper than it had been the previous night. She rose quickly from her chair, ignoring the protest of her stiff muscles as she leaned over him anxiously.

"Edwin?" she called softly, hardly daring to hope yet unable to suppress the tremor of anticipation in her voice.

This time, his eyes opened fully, though they still carried the weight of extreme fatigue. He blinked several times, as if struggling to bring the world into focus, before his gaze finally settled on her face with a flash of recognition that made her heart soar.

"Madeline," he murmured, his voice rough from disuse but carrying an unmistakable note of affection that brought tears to her eyes.

Relief crashed over her like a physical wave, and she clasped his hand more tightly between both of hers, treasuring the fact that it felt cooler than before. "You're awake," she managed to say, her smile trembling as she fought to control her overwhelming emotions. "Truly awake this time."

When he attempted to push himself up against the pillows, she quickly but gently pressed him back down with a hand on his chest. "No, you mustn't strain yourself," she admonished softly. "You need to preserve your strength and rest."

"How long have I...?" he began to ask, but his voice gave out before he could complete the question.

"A day and a night," she informed him, reaching for a cup of water. "You've had us all sick with worry, especially me. I don't think I've ever been more frightened."

Edwin's lips curved into that familiar, gentle smile she had feared she might never see again, though it was but a shadow of its usual brightness. "Always... making trouble," he managed to say, his voice barely more than a whisper. "Causing you... concern."

Madeline couldn't help but laugh softly, even as tears of relief sprang to her eyes. "You're absolutely impossible," she said, her voice thick with emotion. "The most impossible man I've ever known."

He squeezed her hand weakly, but his gaze remained steady on her face despite his obvious exhaustion, filled with a depth of feeling that made her breath catch. "Thank you," he whispered, the words carrying a significance far beyond their simple meaning.

"For what?" she asked softly, unconsciously reaching out to brush a stray lock of dark hair from his forehead – a gesture that had become familiar over her long vigil.

"For staying," he replied simply, those two words somehow conveying all the gratitude, affection, and understanding that filled his heart.

Her chest tightened almost painfully, and she could only nod in response, finding herself completely unable to speak past the enormous lump of emotion that had formed in her throat. In that moment, as the first true rays of morning sunlight began to pierce the gloom, Madeline knew with absolute certainty that she would have stayed forever if necessary.

Chapter Twelve

Edwin's recovery progressed with the same determined steadiness that characterised everything about him, though to Madeline's anxious eyes, it seemed unbearably slow. Each passing day brought with it small but precious victories that she catalogued carefully in her heart – his fever finally broke, leaving his skin cool to the touch for the first time in days; his appetite gradually returned, though he initially protested at the simple fare the doctor prescribed; and most heartening of all, the healthy colour began to creep back into his cheeks, replacing the alarming pallor that had haunted her dreams. Through it all, Madeline maintained her vigil by his bedside, her own exhaustion rendered insignificant by her fierce determination to see him fully restored to health.

The doctor continued his regular visits, his stern demeanour gradually softening from grim concern to cautious optimism as Edwin's condition improved. "He's remarkably fortunate," he observed one crisp morning, his practiced fingers pressed against Edwin's wrist as he monitored his patient's strengthening pulse. "I've seen far too many in his condition succumb to the fever. It seems someone – or something – was watching over him with particular care."

Madeline's eyes met Edwin's across the room, and she felt a faint smile tugging at her lips despite her weariness. She couldn't deny the profound relief that flooded through her entire being each time she witnessed the light of awareness returning to his eyes, growing stronger with each passing day.

As time pressed forward, Edwin slowly regained enough strength to sit upright in bed, supported by an impressive arrangement of pillows that Madeline meticulously adjusted every so often. The servants brought carefully prepared meals – bowls of rich, nourishing broth and slices of fresh bread from the manor's kitchen – and Madeline ensured he ate every bite, gently but firmly scolding him for his persistent attempts to do more than his recovering body could manage.

"You do realise you're not actually invincible, don't you?" she chided one particularly trying afternoon, catching him in yet another attempt to rise from his bed without assistance.

"I'm beginning to suspect you rather enjoy ordering me about," Edwin replied, his eyes twinkling with barely suppressed mischief despite his weakness.

"Well, someone has to keep you from your own worst impulses," she shot back, though she couldn't quite suppress the fond smile that betrayed her true feelings.

This playful interaction became an integral part of their daily routine, providing a welcome respite from the bleakness of the winter world that continued to rage beyond the manor's walls. Madeline found herself treasuring these moments more than she dared admit – the warm richness of Edwin's laughter, the way his mere presence seemed to fill even the grandest room with vitality and purpose.

Yet as his health steadily improved, Madeline became increasingly aware of a new tension developing between them, delicate and charged. She felt it in Edwin's gaze when it lingered on her face while he thought she wasn't looking, in the electric current that seemed to pass between them when their hands accidentally brushed, and in the way neither of them seemed willing to break these moments of contact once they occurred.

One evening, as she moved about the room performing her usual tasks of straightening and tidying, Edwin's voice cut through the comfortable silence, carrying an unusual note of gravity. "Madeline, would you sit with me for a moment?"

She turned towards him, surprised by the serious undertone in his request. "Of course," she replied, settling herself in the chair that had become almost an extension of her own body over the past weeks.

For several long moments, Edwin remained silent, his hands clasped tightly in his lap as if wrestling with some internal struggle. When he finally raised his eyes to meet hers, his expression was carefully composed, yet somehow more vulnerable than she had ever seen it.

"There's something I need to say to you," he began, his voice carrying the weight of carefully considered words.

Madeline's heart began to race beneath her bodice, and she found herself gripping the edges of her chair, as if seeking an anchor in suddenly turbulent waters. "What is it?" she asked.

Edwin hesitated for a breath, then reached across the space between them to take her hand in his, his touch warm and reassuringly steady. "You've done more for me than I could ever hope to repay, Madeline. Not just these past weeks of care and devotion, though Heaven knows that debt alone is beyond measure. It's everything about you – your unwavering strength, your boundless kindness, your fierce determination. You've given me hope when I believed all hope had abandoned me entirely."

Her breath caught painfully in her throat as she struggled to form words. "Edwin, please..."

"No, let me finish," he insisted gently, a soft smile tempering the intensity of his gaze. "I'm well aware of the barriers that exist between us – the artificial divisions that society would never allow us to forget. But after everything we've endured together, I find I can no longer pretend that these obstacles hold any real meaning for me."

Madeline stared at him, her heart thundering so violently in her chest that she was certain he must be able to hear its frantic rhythm in the quiet room.

"I love you," Edwin declared, his voice unwavering despite the raw vulnerability evident in his eyes. "I love you with a depth that defies all reason and propriety, and I find I no longer have any interest in what the world might think of that truth. You are all that matters to me now."

For what felt like an eternity, Madeline remained frozen, too overwhelmed to respond. She had dreamed of hearing those words, had imagined this moment in the quiet hours of her vigil, but now that they hung in the air between them, she found herself paralysed by the magnitude of their meaning. The enormity of his confession settled over her like a mantle, simultaneously thrilling and terrifying in its implications.

"Edwin," she finally managed, her voice trembling with emotion, "you can't possibly know what you're saying. You've been ill, and your judgment..."

"I know precisely what I'm saying," he interrupted with gentle firmness. "In fact, I've never been more certain of anything in all my life."

Tears welled in her eyes, and she shook her head in automatic protest, years of ingrained social consciousness rising to the surface. "But what of your family? Your position? Your good name? They would never accept someone of my standing."

"Then let them live with their disapproval," Edwin declared with unexpected vehemence, his grip on her hand tightening. "I've spent my entire life trying to live up to their impossible expectations, allowing myself to be caged by their rigid notions of propriety. And what has it brought me? A gilded prison, surrounded by people who care more about maintaining appearances than pursuing genuine happiness or truth."

Madeline felt her carefully constructed resolve beginning to crumble beneath the enormity of his impassioned words. Every fibre of her being yearned to believe him, to trust in the depth and sincerity of his feelings, but the doubt that had been her constant companion throughout her life refused to release its hold entirely.

"I don't know if I can be what you need," she confessed, her voice barely audible even in the quiet room. "I don't know if I can give you the life you deserve."

Edwin leaned closer, his eyes searching hers with an intensity that seemed to peer directly into her soul. "My dearest Madeline," he said softly, "you've already given me something far more precious than anything I could have hoped for – you've given me a reason to truly live."

The room fell into a charged silence, broken only by the gentle crackling of the fire in the hearth and the rapid beating of their hearts. Madeline felt herself being pulled towards him by an invisible force, every rational argument she had prepared crumbling in the face of their undeniable connection.

Then, before her ever-present caution could reassert itself, she closed the remaining distance between them and pressed her lips to his in a kiss that contained all the words she couldn't bring herself to say.

The kiss was gentle and uncertain at first, as delicate as a butterfly's wing and just as liable to take flight at any moment. But as Edwin's hand came up to cup her face with infinite tenderness, she felt a warmth bloom in her chest, a profound sense of belonging that chased away both the physical cold of winter and the emotional chill of her long-held fears.

When they finally drew apart, Edwin's smile was radiant with joy and mischief. "Does this mean you'll finally stop arguing with me about everything?" he asked, his thumb brushing away the tears that had escaped down her cheek.

Madeline couldn't help but laugh, even as more tears traced silver paths down her face.

"Not even in your wildest dreams," she declared, her voice thick with emotion but carrying a note of her usual spirit.

As she looked into Edwin's eyes, bright with love and promise, she finally allowed herself to believe that they might find a way to defy the odds that stood against them.

Chapter Thirteen

The kiss lingered in Madeline's mind like a phantom touch, haunting her thoughts long after the sweetness of the moment had faded into memory. As Edwin lay peacefully sleeping that evening, his chest rising and falling gently, she maintained her vigil beside him, her mind a tempestuous sea of conflicting emotions. Every detail of their encounter refused to release its hold on her consciousness: the tenderness of his words, the gentle pressure of his touch against her skin, the unwavering intensity of his gaze that seemed to pierce through every defence she had ever built. All of it felt like something from a dream, too perfect to exist in the harsh light of reality. And yet, undeniably, impossibly, it was real.

But that reality brought with it a fear that pressed against her chest with each passing moment. The world that existed beyond the protective walls of their small sanctuary was not a forgiving one. It was a realm of rigid social hierarchies and merciless judgment, where class stood as an insurmountable barrier that no amount of love, no matter how pure or passionate, could easily overcome. The thought of Edwin facing ostracism from his family – the very people who had shaped his world since birth – sent waves of sick dread coursing through her veins. She couldn't bear the idea of his proud family name being dragged through the mud, tarnished and besmirched, all because he had dared to love someone so far beneath his station.

Through the long hours of the night, she maintained her position by his bedside, drifting in and out of fitful slumber in the unyielding wooden chair. Her dreams, when they came, were fragmented things filled with shadowy figures and whispered condemnations. When consciousness finally returned to her, she found the fire had dwindled to barely glowing embers, and the first tentative rays of dawn were beginning to penetrate the heavy curtains, casting the room in a pale, ethereal light. Edwin remained lost in sleep, but his breathing had taken on a strong, steady rhythm that spoke of healing, and the healthy colour that had returned to his cheeks brought her more joy than she dared to express.

The relief that flooded through her system was immediate and all-consuming, yet even this moment of profound gratitude was quickly sobered by the reality bearing down upon her shoulders. She knew she couldn't continue hiding within this precious bubble of stolen happiness forever.

The morning progressed, and with it came the return of the doctor, his keen eyes sharp as polished steel as they scrutinised Edwin's condition. She watched anxiously as he conducted his examination with methodical precision, her heart catching at every flicker of emotion that crossed his face.

"Well," the doctor announced at last, taking a step back and folding his arms across his chest with an air of professional satisfaction. "I believe we can safely say our young nobleman has successfully weathered the storm. The fever has broken completely, and his strength appears to be returning at an admirable rate. With proper rest and continued care, I would estimate he'll be back on his feet within a week's time."

The wave of relief that washed over Madeline was so profound it made her lightheaded, though years of practiced restraint helped her maintain an outwardly composed demeanour. "Your skill and dedication have been invaluable, Doctor. We both owe you a tremendous debt of gratitude."

The doctor acknowledged her words with a professional nod as he began gathering his various instruments. "Gratitude is all well and good, but what I require now is adherence to my instructions. Don't allow him to push himself too quickly – I'm well acquainted with the temperament of young noblemen. They're invariably eager to return to their usual activities long before their bodies are truly prepared for such exertion."

A weak chuckle emanated from the bed where Edwin lay. "You have my solemn word, Doctor. I shall endeavour to be the most cooperative patient you've ever treated."

With a final knowing look that suggested

he'd heard similar promises before, the doctor took his leave, allowing silence to descend once more over the room like a gentle blanket.

Madeline turned her attention back to Edwin, only to find him already watching her with that soft, knowing smile that never failed to make her heart skip a beat. The tenderness in his expression made her feel simultaneously seen and exposed in a way that both thrilled and terrified her.

"What is it?" she asked, feeling heat rise to her cheeks under the warmth of his steady gaze.

"The dark circles beneath your eyes tell quite a story," he observed, his voice gentle with concern. "You've been tormenting yourself with worry over my condition, haven't you?"

"How could I not?" she responded, crossing her arms defensively across her chest as if to shield her heart from the vulnerability of the moment. "You gave everyone quite the fright with your illness. For a time, we weren't certain..." She couldn't bring herself to complete the terrible thought.

Edwin extended his hand towards her, and when she placed her fingers in his palm, the warmth of his touch sent shivers of awareness through her entire body. "I'm deeply sorry to have caused you such distress," he murmured, his voice rich with sincerity. "But I cannot express how grateful I am to have had you by my side throughout this ordeal. I doubt anyone else would have shown such dedication or tenderness in caring for me."

Madeline felt her throat constrict with emotion, the raw honesty in his voice threatening to crumble the careful walls she'd constructed. "You possess far too much charm for your own good," she managed to say, though she couldn't quite suppress the smile that tugged at the corners of her mouth.

"Perhaps," he acknowledged with a hint of playfulness, his thumb tracing delicate patterns across her knuckles that sent sparks of electricity racing up her arm. "But only because it seems to have such a delightful effect on you."

With gentle reluctance, she withdrew her

hand from his grasp, feeling the loss of contact like a physical ache. Her smile faded as reality once again intruded upon their moment of connection. "Edwin, we need to have a serious discussion about what the future holds."

His expression sobered immediately, and he gave her a solemn nod. "Yes, I suppose we do."

Madeline rose and began to pace the length of the room, her skirts swishing softly against the wooden floorboards. "Your family," she began, forcing herself to voice the fears that had been plaguing her. "They will never accept or approve of... whatever this is between us. You must know that."

Edwin's gaze followed her movement, his eyes never leaving her face. "Their approval or lack thereof means nothing to me."

"But it should!" she exclaimed, whirling to face him with unexpected intensity. "Your name, your position in society, your reputation – these things are the very foundation of your family's existence. If you were to cast it all aside for someone of my standing..." The words caught in her throat, too painful to voice fully.

"Someone of your standing?" he repeated, his brow furrowing with obvious displeasure at her choice of words. "Madeline, you've become everything to me. The rest of it – titles, wealth, social position: it's all meaningless in comparison."

She shook her head vigorously, feeling frustration bubble up from deep within her chest. "You say such things now, here in this room where the world can't touch us. But what about later? What happens when the full consequence of your choices crashes down upon you? When society turns its back on you, when doors begin closing in your face, when whispers follow you through every room – all because of me?"

With visible effort, Edwin pushed himself into a more upright position, wincing slightly at the movement but maintaining his determined expression. "The world as I knew it has already crumbled around me," he declared, his voice carrying a steel-like conviction. "This plague has stolen so much – beloved friends, cherished family members, even the basic trust I once held in my own household. You, Madeline, are the only thing that still feels authentic and true. The only thing that gives me the strength to face whatever comes next."

His impassioned words struck her with physical force, leaving her momentarily breathless and unable to form a coherent response. Every fibre of her being yearned to surrender to the safety and warmth of his love, to believe that it could be enough to overcome the obstacles that lay before them. But the fear remained, an ever-present shadow that clouded her hope with doubt.

"What if I'm not enough?" she asked, the words carrying all the insecurities that had plagued her since their feelings for each other had first become apparent.

Edwin's expression softened with such tenderness that it made her heart ache. He extended his hand towards her once more, and when she hesitated, he spoke with gentle insistence. "Come here, Madeline."

After a moment's internal struggle, she crossed the room and perched carefully on the edge of his bed. He took both her hands in his, his grip providing an anchor of warmth and stability that seemed to steady her tumultuous emotions.

"You are more than enough," he assured her, each word laden with quiet but unshakeable conviction. "You are everything I never knew I was searching for, and if the world cannot recognise your worth, then I want no part of that world."

Tears welled up in her eyes, and she turned her face away, ashamed of displaying such vulnerability. "I'm terrified," she confessed, her voice trembling with the admission. "Not just of what might happen, but of how much I want this despite knowing better."

Chapter Fourteen

The days that followed their conversation unfolded in a delicate dance of careful planning and precious moments stolen in the relative sanctuary of Edwin's chambers. Though uncertainty continued to loom over them like a persistent shadow, Madeline found herself increasingly buoyed by Edwin's unwavering determination and quiet strength. In their intimate conversations, he spoke with passionate conviction about their future together, painting vivid pictures with his words of a life far removed from the stifling confines of Ryehaven – a place where the rigid barriers of social class would hold no power over them, and where even the dark memory of the plague that had brought them together would fade into distant memory.

Yet even as Edwin's health showed marked improvement with each passing day,

Madeline couldn't shake the sensation that something would crush their fragile dreams. It was during one of these tension-filled days, as Edwin attempted his first tentative venture beyond the confines of his room, that the reality they had been desperately trying to outrun finally caught up with them. Madeline supported him carefully as they navigated the grand staircase together, his arm draped heavily across her shoulders as he leaned on her for support. With each step, she could feel the tension in his muscles, could hear the way he gritted his teeth against the discomfort, but his determination to succeed was almost tangible in the air between them.

"You've proven to be far more stubborn than I initially gave you credit for," she observed with a gentle, teasing smile, trying to distract him from the strain of their slow descent.

"I had an excellent teacher in that regard," Edwin responded, his voice tight with exertion but still managing to convey a wealth of affection.

Their careful progress was suddenly interrupted as they reached the bottom of the stairs, where the distinct sound of voices carried from the direction of the drawing room. Edwin's entire body tensed beside her, his grip tightening instinctively around her arm with enough force to nearly make her wince.

"What's wrong?" Madeline asked, her eyes following his frozen gaze with growing concern.

Before Edwin could formulate a response, the door to the drawing room swung open with an ominous creak, and a tall, imposing figure stepped into the hallway. Lord Hale, Edwin's father, cut an intimidating figure in his immaculately tailored dark suit, his sharp, aristocratic features carved with lines of immediate and obvious disapproval. His penetrating gaze swept over Edwin first, assessing his son's weakened state with clear displeasure, before shifting to Madeline. She watched as his eyes narrowed dangerously, the moment of recognition dawning across his face.

"What is the meaning of this disgraceful display?" Lord Hale demanded, his voice cold and cutting.

Madeline felt her stomach plummet to her feet, but beside her, Edwin somehow managed to straighten his posture, meeting his father's accusatory stare with a calm defiance that spoke of years of similar confrontations. "Father," he acknowledged evenly, his tone carefully neutral. "This is certainly unexpected. I thought you were determined to remain sequestered in your study until the threat of contagion had passed completely."

"And yet, here I stand," Lord Hale replied, his words sharp enough to draw blood. "Now, I expect an immediate answer to my question. Who is this woman, and why is she presuming to hang upon you like some common nursemaid?"

Madeline felt her throat constrict as she opened her mouth to defend herself, but Edwin's voice cut through the tension first, steady and unwavering. "This is Madeline," he declared with quiet dignity. "She is the sole reason I'm standing here before you today. When others fled in fear of the plague, she stayed by my side and tended to me with unwavering dedication."

Lord Hale's expression darkened further, his features twisting with barely contained fury as he turned the full force of his attention to Madeline. "Is that so?" he drawled, each word dripping with thinly veiled contempt. "And what exactly do you expect to gain from this remarkable... display of kindness?"

The cruel insinuation in his tone sent waves of heat rushing to Madeline's cheeks, but she forced herself to stand tall under his withering gaze. "I expect nothing whatsoever from you or your family, my lord," she responded with as much dignity as she could muster. "My only desire was to help someone in desperate need."

"Help," Lord Hale echoed, the word twisted with derision in his mouth. "How remarkably noble of you. However, let me be perfectly clear about this situation, young woman: whatever connection you believe you have fostered with my son ends at this precise moment. I trust I make myself understood?"

"That is quite enough," Edwin interrupted, his voice cutting through the tension with unexpected force. "I will not stand here and allow you to speak to Madeline as though she were some kind of opportunistic fortune hunter. She is the woman I love, Father, and I absolutely refuse to let you or anyone else address her with such blatant disrespect."

Lord Hale's eyes widened perceptibly, his momentary shock quickly transforming into a towering rage that seemed to fill the entire hallway. "Love?" he said the word as though it was poison. "Have you completely lost what remaining sense you possess, Edwin? Can you not comprehend the magnitude of the scandal this... this liaison would bring down upon our family name?"

"The family name means nothing to me in comparison to her," Edwin declared, his voice rising with passion. "I care for Madeline more than I have ever cared for social standing or reputation."

The grand hallway fell into a charged silence that seemed to crackle with unspoken tensions. Madeline's heart thundered against her ribs, her emotions a whirling maelstrom of fear, gratitude, and stunned disbelief at Edwin's public declaration.

Lord Hale stared at his son as though seeing

him for the first time, his jaw clenched so tightly that a muscle twitched visibly beneath his skin. "You are nothing but a love-struck fool," he pronounced with glacial coldness. "And I promise you, you will live to bitterly regret this moment of madness."

Without deigning to wait for a response, he turned on his heel and strode back into the drawing room, the door slamming behind him with enough force to rattle the nearby windows.

With trembling hands and a racing mind, Madeline carefully helped Edwin navigate the return journey to his chambers. Once there, she guided him to sit on the edge of his bed, ensuring he was comfortably settled before sinking into the nearby chair, her legs suddenly too weak to support her weight.

"Well, I'd say that went splendidly," Edwin remarked with forced lightness, though the smile he attempted failed to reach his troubled eyes.

Madeline shot him an incredulous look, her nerves still raw from the confrontation. "How can you possibly maintain such composure?

Your father clearly despises everything about me and what I represent."

"He doesn't know you," Edwin countered with gentle firmness. "And even if he took the time to discover your true nature, I doubt it would sway his opinion. My father has always been far more concerned with maintaining appearances than with understanding the hearts of actual people."

"But what if his fears are justified?" she burst out. "What if this dream we're chasing is truly impossible? What if..."

"Madeline," Edwin interrupted, extending his hand to take hers with quiet authority. "Please, look at me properly."

After a moment's hesitation, she raised her eyes to meet his steady gaze, finding in their depths the same unwavering conviction that had first captured her heart.

"We will find our way through this," he stated with quiet but absolute certainty. "Whatever obstacles we must overcome, whatever price we must pay. Do you trust in that? Do you trust in me?"

She swallowed hard against the lump in her throat, the pure sincerity in his expression cutting through the tangled web of her doubts like a shaft of sunlight through storm clouds. "I do trust you," she whispered, the words like a sacred vow.

"Then that is all we truly need," he declared, his grip on her hand tightening with reassuring pressure. "Everything else is merely detail."

Madeline managed a small nod, though she couldn't entirely banish the fear that continued to coil around her heart. She wanted desperately to believe in Edwin's words, to place her faith completely in the strength of their love. But the echo of Lord Hale's cruel pronouncements lingered in her mind like a bitter aftertaste, a stark reminder of the formidable obstacles that still stood between them and any hope of happiness together.

Chapter Fifteen

Madeline maintained her vigil beside Edwin's bed long after he had succumbed to a fitful, restless sleep. The fire in the ornate hearth provided the room's only illumination, its flames dancing and crackling softly as they cast ever-shifting shadows across the richly papered walls. Despite the fire's steady warmth, she couldn't shake the chill that had settled over her in the wake of their confrontation with Lord Hale. His cutting words continued to echo through her mind with ruthless persistence, each repetition serving as a stark reminder of the seemingly insurmountable social chasm that lay between her and the man she had grown to love.

She had never been naive enough to believe their path would be an easy one, but the reality felt far worse than she had prepared herself to bear. Edwin's unwavering love and steadfast determination gave her a measure of courage she had never known she possessed, yet his father's obvious disdain pressed down upon her shoulders like a physical burden.

Moving carefully so as not to disturb Edwin's much-needed rest, Madeline rose from her chair and crossed to the frost-etched window. Outside, snow was falling in delicate, silent flakes, gradually transforming the expansive manor grounds into a pristine white landscape that seemed to glow with an ethereal light in the growing darkness. For a precious moment, she allowed herself to indulge in a forbidden fantasy – a different life, one where she and Edwin could stroll hand in hand through the freshly fallen snow without fear of judgment or consequence, their love as pure and unblemished as the winter landscape before her.

But such gentle dreams held no power in the harsh light of reality, where the world showed little mercy to those who dared to challenge its rigid social order.

A soft, hesitant knock at the chamber door yanked her abruptly from her wistful reverie. Turning, she found one of the manor's younger maids hovering uncertainly in the doorway, her expression caught between sympathy and trepidation.

"Miss Madeline," the maid whispered, her voice barely carrying across the room, "Lord Hale has requested your immediate presence in his private study."

Madeline felt her stomach contract painfully. "At this hour?"

The maid nodded, wringing her hands nervously in her apron. "He was most insistent, miss. Said it was a matter of great urgency that couldn't wait until morning."

Madeline cast an anxious glance towards Edwin's sleeping form, watching the steady rise and fall of his chest for several heartbeats. Finding strength in his peaceful expression, she squared her shoulders and followed the maid into the manor's dimly lit corridors, their footsteps muffled by the thick carpets that lined the floors.

Upon reaching the imposing oak door of Lord Hale's study, the maid opened it with practiced quietness before stepping aside with a small curtsey, gesturing for Madeline to enter the lion's den alone.

Lord Hale cut an austere figure as he stood by the frost-covered window, his back rigid and his hands clasped tightly behind him in a pose that spoke of barely contained tension. The room itself seemed to reflect its master's mood – dark and oppressive, illuminated only by the dying embers in the fireplace and the ethereal glow of the falling snow beyond the glass.

"You summoned me, my lord," Madeline said, forcing her voice to remain steady despite the nervous flutter of her heart.

Lord Hale turned with deliberate slowness, his penetrating gaze fixing upon her with the intensity of a hawk studying its prey. "Close the door," he commanded, his tone clipped and brooking no argument.

Madeline complied, the soft click of the latch seeming to echo ominously in the charged silence of the study.

"Sit," he directed curtly, motioning towards a high-backed leather chair positioned near the dying fire.

After a moment's hesitation, Madeline lowered herself into the indicated seat, folding her hands tightly in her lap to hide their slight tremor. She lifted her chin and met his calculating stare, determined not to let him see the fear that threatened to overwhelm her composure.

"You strike me as an intelligent woman," Lord Hale began, his tone carefully measured but carrying an underlying edge of steel. "Therefore, I will not insult your intelligence by pretending this is a conversation between equals. You must surely recognise that whatever... attachment you believe you have formed with my son is destined for failure."

Madeline's jaw tightened at his deliberate emphasis on their social inequality, but she held her tongue, waiting for him to continue.

"Edwin bears the name of Hale," Lord Hale continued, beginning to pace with measured steps before the fireplace. "It is a name that carries with it not merely wealth, but centuries of history, tradition, and responsibility. It is not a legacy to be carelessly tarnished by scandal or youthful foolishness."

"Edwin is more than just his family name," Madeline responded, keeping her voice calm but allowing a note of firmness to enter it. "He is his own person, with the right to determine his own destiny."

Lord Hale's eyes narrowed dangerously at her interruption. "His destiny, as you put it, does not include you."

The words struck her terribly, but Madeline forced herself to maintain her composure. "With all due respect, my lord, that decision belongs to Edwin alone, not to you or anyone else."

A flicker of something – perhaps rage, perhaps grudging respect – passed briefly across his aristocratic features before his expression smoothed once more into careful neutrality. "You display remarkable boldness for someone in your position," he observed with disdain. "But courage alone will not shield you from the consequences of your actions." He stepped closer, using his height to loom over her in a clear attempt at intimidation. "If you harbour any genuine feeling for my son," he continued, his voice dropping to a dangerous whisper, "you will pack your belongings tonight and leave this manor, never to return. Spare him the disgrace of destroying everything his ancestors have built by aligning himself with someone so very far beneath his station."

Madeline felt her chest constrict painfully at his words, but she refused to let them break her spirit. "If I were to leave," she challenged, maintaining steady eye contact despite her racing heart, "do you truly believe that would be the end of it? Do you imagine Edwin would simply forget my existence and conform to your wishes?"

Lord Hale's expression hardened to granite. "He would have no choice in the matter."

The silence that followed his declaration was suffocating in its intensity. Madeline felt her resolve waver for a moment, but she forced herself to rise from the chair, standing straight and proud despite her trembling knees.

"I understand your concerns for your family's reputation, my lord," she said, struggling to keep her voice steady. "But Edwin deserves the chance to live his life according to his own conscience and heart. If you truly love your son, you will grant him the freedom to make that choice for himself."

Lord Hale's jaw clenched visibly, but he offered no response to her words.

Madeline turned and walked from the study with as much dignity as she could muster, but the moment she crossed the threshold into the empty hallway, she sagged against the wall, her knees threatening to buckle beneath her as the full intensity of the confrontation crashed over her.

She couldn't be certain whether she had emerged victorious or defeated from their encounter, but one truth remained crystal clear: Lord Hale would not surrender his son's future without waging a bitter war for it.

When she finally returned to Edwin's chambers, she found him awake and alert, his worried eyes scanning her face the moment she appeared in the doorway.

"Where have you been?" he asked, concern evident in every syllable. "I woke and found you gone."

"Your father requested my presence in his study," she explained, crossing the room to perch on the edge of his bed.

Edwin's expression darkened immediately. "What did he say to you?"

Madeline hesitated for a moment before taking his hand in both of hers, drawing comfort from the familiar warmth of his touch. "He wants me to leave the manor," she admitted softly. "He sees me as a threat to everything the Hale name represents – your position, your future, your family's standing in society."

Edwin's face clouded with anger. "I need to speak with him immediately."

"No," Madeline interjected quickly, tightening her grip on his hand. "Please, not yet. You're still recovering your strength, and I couldn't bear to see you risk your health over this confrontation."

He released a heavy sigh, his fingers interlacing with hers in a gesture of silent support. "Madeline, you could never be a threat to me or my future. You're the very reason I have a future at all."

She managed a wan smile, though her worries were predominant. "We'll find a way through this," she murmured, trying to convince herself as much as him.

Edwin nodded solemnly, but she could see the lingering tension in his eyes, the worry that matched her own.

Chapter Sixteen

The late afternoon sunlight filtered through the frost-etched windows of Edwin's chamber, casting long shadows across the richly carpeted floor. Madeline sat in her usual chair beside Edwin's bed as he sat fully upright, supported by an arrangement of pillows against the ornate headboard.

Her hands rested in her lap, her fingers wrapping around a loose thread on her sleeve as Edwin's earlier words echoed in her mind. He had been insistent, his tone leaving no room for argument. "You belong here," he had said with a conviction that had made her heart ache. "I'll not have you banished from my home as though you were some trespasser. Whatever my father thinks, his will does not dictate my life."

Though his determination had been undeniable, it had done little to soothe the unease coiling in Madeline's chest. Every glance she exchanged with a servant, every creak of the floorboards in the hall, reminded her of Lord Hale's looming presence and disapproving gaze. Yet how could she defy Edwin when his desire for her to stay was so clear? It felt only natural to yield to his wishes, even if doing so meant inviting the ire of his father.

"I feel that I might be able to return to my normal activities within the week," Edwin remarked, his voice carrying none of the weakness that had characterised it during his illness. "Though I suspect you'll still insist on monitoring my every move."

Madeline allowed herself a small smile, grateful for these quiet moments they could share. "Someone has to ensure you don't immediately overexert yourself. I know how stubborn you can be."

Their gentle conversation was interrupted by a sharp knock at the door. Before either could respond, it swung open to reveal Martha, one of the senior housemaids. Her face was pale, her usual composure notably disturbed.

"Master Edwin," she said, her voice trembling slightly. "You're needed immediately. It's... it's your father, sir."

Madeline felt Edwin stiffen beside her. "What about my father?"

Martha wrung her hands in her apron. "He's taken ill, sir. Very ill. The doctor suspects it's the plague. He's asking for you."

The colour drained from Edwin's face as he pushed himself to his feet. Madeline rose automatically to steady him, though he had regained enough strength to stand unaided. Their eyes met briefly, volumes of unspoken understanding passing between them.

Together, they followed Martha through the manor's winding corridors. When they reached Lord Hale's chambers, Madeline gently squeezed Edwin's hand before releasing it.

"I'll wait here," she said softly.

He nodded, then disappeared into his father's room, leaving Madeline alone in the corridor with her thoughts.

***

The days that followed settled into a strange pattern. Madeline remained at the manor, providing what comfort she could to Edwin between his vigils at his father's bedside. She kept her distance from Lord Hale's chambers out of respect for his previously stated wishes, but her heart ached for Edwin each time he emerged, looking more worn and worried than before.

It was nearly a week later when everything changed. The sun had just begun to set, painting the manor's windows in shades of amber and gold, when another servant appeared at Edwin's door. His expression told Madeline everything she needed to know before he even spoke.

"Your father is asking for you both, sir," the servant said quietly, his eyes flickering briefly to Madeline.

Edwin's head snapped up in surprise. "Both of us?"

"Yes, sir. He was very specific."

Once again, Madeline found herself walking the now-familiar path to Lord Hale's chambers, her hand clasped tightly in Edwin's. This time, however, they both entered the room.

The sight that greeted them made Madeline's breath catch in her throat. Lord Hale lay propped up in his massive four-poster bed, his once-imposing frame now terribly diminished by illness. The plague had ravaged him with shocking speed, leaving him pale and drawn, his sharp features made even more severe by the shadows of approaching death.

"Edwin," he called weakly, his voice barely more than a whisper. "And Madeline. Come closer, both of you."

They approached the bedside, Edwin maintaining his grip on Madeline's hand as though drawing strength from her presence. Lord Hale's eyes, though clouded with fever, remained alert as they studied the couple before him.

"I have been..." he paused, fighting for breath, "perhaps too rigid in my thinking. This illness has taught me much about what truly matters in life."

Edwin leaned forward slightly. "Father, you don't need to..."

Lord Hale raised a trembling hand to silence him. "Let me finish, son. I don't have much time." He turned his gaze to Madeline. "Young woman, I judged you harshly, by standards that perhaps... perhaps deserve to be questioned. I was so focused on preserving our family's position that I forgot what it means to be truly noble."

Madeline felt tears pricking at her eyes as Lord Hale continued, his voice growing weaker with each word.

"The way you cared for my son, the courage you've shown in the face of my disapproval – these are qualities worth more than any title or fortune," he said, coughing, the sound rattling in his chest. "Edwin, I have watched you stand firm in your convictions, defending your love despite everything. You have shown me that there is more to life than the narrow path I tried to force you down."

"Thank you, Father," Edwin said, his voice thick with emotion.

Lord Hale's lips curved in a faint smile. "I still believe in tradition, in the importance of our family name. But perhaps... perhaps it is time for that tradition to evolve. To become something stronger, something more meaningful."

His eyes found Madeline's once more. "Take care of him," he whispered. "Love him as you have shown you can. And know that you have my blessing, for whatever that may still be worth."

Madeline couldn't speak past the lump in her throat, but she nodded, tears flowing freely down her cheeks. Lord Hale seemed satisfied with this response, his expression softening as he turned back to his son.

"Edwin," he said weakly, his voice barely audible now. "I am proud of you. Remember that."

They were his last words. As the last rays of sunlight faded from the windows, Lord Hale's eyes drifted shut, and his breathing gradually slowed until it finally ceased altogether. Edwin's grip on Madeline's hand tightened painfully, but she didn't pull away. Instead, she drew closer to him, offering what comfort she could in the face of his loss.

Epilogue

The day of the wedding dawned bright and clear. The early summer sun cast a golden glow over the town of Ryehaven. The once sombre church bell rang out from the tower, its sound filling the air with a newfound joy, carrying far and wide as people gathered to witness the union. The plague that had haunted their lives through the long, bleak winter had finally receded, its cruel grip having let go by late spring. And now, although there were still the dreaded losses of a harsh winter to grieve, as the warmth of summer touched the earth, the promise of a brighter future was embodied.

Madeline stood in the small room behind the church, her hands trembling slightly as she adjusted the simple white gown she wore. It was not extravagant by any means, but it was just right – sewn with love by the town seamstress and adorned with delicate lace. It was a humble garment, but beautiful in its simplicity.

"Are you nervous?" Mary asked, standing behind her and helping pin a flower into her hair.

"A little," Madeline admitted, though her smile betrayed her excitement.

"You'll be fine," Mary said reassuringly. "Edwin adores you. And the whole town loves you both."

Madeline nodded, her heart swelling with gratitude. She took a deep breath, steadying herself as the door creaked open.

"It's time," Father Gregory said, his kind eyes crinkling as he smiled.

Madeline stepped into the church, her breath catching as she saw Edwin waiting for her at the altar. He stood tall and proud, his hair combed neatly, and his eyes shining with a warmth that chased away all her worries. His expression was one of quiet strength, a man who had endured much, yet had come through it with his heart unbroken. As

Madeline walked towards him, the guests rose to their feet in a show of support, and she felt her nerves begin to melt away.

When she reached Edwin, he took her hands in his, his touch steady and sure. "You're breathtaking," he said, his voice low enough for only her to hear.

Madeline smiled, her cheeks warming. "And you're impossibly handsome," she whispered back.

Father Gregory began the ceremony, his voice steady and filled with quiet reverence. The vows they exchanged were simple but heartfelt, each word honouring their journey together, and the healing that had come with it.

When the time came to seal their union, Edwin leaned down, his lips brushing hers in a kiss that was both tender and filled with promise. The church erupted into cheers, the bell ringing once more to celebrate the beginning of the happy couple's new life together.